SUICIDE SNIPER

Hickok could hear the jeep motor sputtering and rumbling as he hurried toward it. He had scant hope of finding the sniper alive.

The assassin unexpectedly rose to his knees, reeling, a torrent of blood pouring from a hole in his cranium. He was fumbling with his right pants pocket.

Hickok held his fire, knowing the sniper would be easy to take. He was ten feet from the jeep when the assassin's hand came into view holding a hand grenade.

Hickok threw himself backward, twisting in midair, but he was a foot from the asphalt when the grenade went off, the thundering blast sending fragments of metal, glass, and pulpy tissue in every direction . . . .

Also in the *Endworld* series:

THE FOX RUN
THIEF RIVER FALLS RUN
TWIN CITIES RUN
KALISPELL RUN
DAKOTA RUN
CITADEL RUN
ARMAGEDDON RUN
DENVER RUN
CAPITAL RUN
NEW YORK RUN
LIBERTY RUN
HOUSTON RUN

ENDWORLD 13
Anaheim Run

David Robbins

LEISURE BOOKS   NEW YORK CITY

Dedicated to . . .
Judy, Joshua, and Megan.
To the memory of Sir Arthur Conan Doyle,
and the occupant of the flat at 221-B Baker Street.

A LEISURE BOOK

Published by

Dorchester Publishing Co., Inc.
276 Fifth Avenue
New York, NY 10001

Copyright©1988 by David Robbins

All rights reserved. No part of this book may be reproduced or transmitted in any form or by any electronic or mechanical means, including photocopying, recording, or by any information storage and retrieval system, without the written permission of the Publisher, except where permitted by law.

Printed in the United States of America

Prologue 1

"Listen!" exclaimed the oldest of the trio, an elderly man with a shock of white hair and gray brows. A strong breeze from the west, from the Pacific Ocean, stirred his brown woolen shirt and baggy green pants. The air was exceptionally chilly along the West Coast, even for January.

"I don't hear nothin'," commented the youngest of the party, a skinny youth barely out of his teens. Brushing his long black hair from his brown eyes, he scanned the vestige of a road they were following to the north. Potholes dotted the buckled asphalt, and the surrounding vegetation served as a verdant wall. The wind seemed to shear right through his blue short-sleeved shirt and black trousers. "There's nothin' out there," he commented.

"I knew we should have stuck to the main roads!" complained the young woman lagging slightly behind the two men. Her shoulder-length black hair was being lashed by the gusts, and her blue pants and blouse provided scant protection from the cold.

"Will you quit gripin', sis!" countered the youth.

"We should have stayed with the main roads!" his sister reiterated. "You know how dangerous it is to stray!" She paused, shivering. "And why didn't we bring an extra set of clothes? Warm clothes!"

"It was nice when we left yesterday," the youth said.

"It's not nice now!" his sister groused.

"Quiet! Both of you!" barked the elderly man.

"What's with you, Grandpa?" the youth demanded. "Everything is cool."

"In more ways than one!" interjected his sister bitterly.

"I tell you there's something out there!" Grandpa insisted.

The youth gazed up at the darkening sky, spying several

stars in the firmament. "Let's find a spot to camp for the night. We'll start a fire. If there's an animal in those woods, a fire will scare it off."

"What if it's not an animal?" the sister asked.

Grandpa glanced at the young woman. "Don't fret none, Tess. We're only about thirty miles from Los Angeles. The damn Raiders don't ordinarily come in this close to the city. They're afraid of running into a Free State patrol."

"But the soldiers only patrol the main roads," Tess noted. "And who knows where the hell we are?"

"I know," Grandpa asserted. "And by this time tomorrow, you'll be safe and sound at your Aunt Betty's."

"We never should have left Rincon Springs," Tess muttered.

"I haven't seen my sister in ten years," Grandpa said. "If your folks were alive, they'd agree this trip was a good idea."

"Grandpa, what's that?" the youth inquired, pointing to the southwest.

Grandpa turned in the indicated direction. Visible above the trees in the distance, reflecting the fading glow of the vanishing sun, was an imposing edifice consisting of white spires and towers with slanted blue roofs. Even from afar, he could distinguish a dilapidated aspect to the structure. "That used to be an amusement park. I forget its name. My father told me once, but that was fifty years ago. Nobody goes there anymore."

"What's an amusement park?" the youth queried.

"I'll tell you all about it later," Grandpa said. "Right now, Johnny, we'd better find a place to camp."

They hastened to the north, their ears alert for any sound from the woods.

"Hey! Look at that!" Johnny cried.

To their left, perhaps 15 yards from the ancient road, was a tumbledown frame house, long since abandoned. The windows had been broken and the front door was dangling from one rusted hinge. Weeds choked the yard and partially covered a cracked cement walk leading up to a collapsed wooden porch.

"How about there?" Johnny questioned.

ANAHEIM RUN

Grandpa stared at the steadily dimming sky. "We don't have any choice. At least there will be a lot of wood we can use for our fire."

"Let's get out of the wind!" Tess urged.

Grandpa, his right hand on the Astra Model 357 strapped to his right hip, took the lead, cautiously advancing along the walk to the house. The sagging green wooden steps creaked as he stepped up to the porch. "Wait here," he directed.

"Be careful!" Tess warned.

Johnny drew his machete from its sheath on his hip. "I wish I was packin' a gun," he commented.

"I wish we'd never taken this shortcut," Tess mentioned.

"You're the one who wanted to reach L.A. as fast as possible," Johnny noted. "Grandpa was just doing you a favor."

"Me and my big mouth," Tess said.

Grandpa skirted the gaping hole in the middle of the porch and sidled closer to the door. He peered into the gloomy interior.

Tess nervously glanced at the nearby trees. "Why is it I feel like something is watching me?"

"Because you're a jerk," Johnny replied.

"Up yours!"

Gandpa disappeared into the house.

"I hope nothing happens to him," Tess said.

"You should of thought of that before," Johnny stated.

"Why the hell are you getting on my case?" Tess inquired angrily.

A branch snapped in the encircling forest.

"What was that?" Tess blurted in alarm.

"Don't crap your pants," Johnny ridiculed her. "It could have just been a rabbit."

"And it could have been a mutant!" Tess rejoined anxiously.

"The mutants have all been killed off from around here," Johnny said. "The wild ones, anyway."

"They've been exterminated close to the cities," Tess declared. "But we're thirty miles from L.A."

"Like Grandpa said," Johnny remarked. "The Raiders

don't come around here anymore, and the same goes for the wild mutants."

"I hope you're right," Tess said.

"Trust me, sis," Johnny stated reassuringly.

"Not on your life," Tess said.

Grandpa appeared in the front doorway. He beckoned for them to join him.

"What's inside?" Johnny asked.

"See for yourselves," Grandpa said.

They entered to find the home had been ravaged, with broken furniture scattered all over the floor. A few cobwebs hung from the ceiling.

"Go on up," Grandpa instructed them, motioning toward a flight of stairs to the right.

Johnny went up first, Tess on his heels. The second floor was in marginally better condition, and there were two chairs and a bed still intact in one of the rooms to the left of the stairs.

"Tess can use the bed," Grandpa said.

"Sleep on that cruddy thing?" Tess griped.

"It's either the bed or the floor," Grandpa told her. "Take your pick."

Tess walked over to the bed and patted the pitiful remnant of a mattress. She coughed as a swirl of dust enshrouded her face.

"We'll be safe on this floor," Grandpa said. "You stay here while I check the kitchen."

"The kitchen?" Johnny repeated quizzically.

"Sometimes you can find old pots and pans in these deserted homes," Grandpa explained. "There might be something I can use to contain a fire. You'll see." He walked off.

Tess sat on the edge of the bed and sighed. "I'm sorry I ever agreed to go see Aunt Betty."

"I'm lookin' forward to gettin' there," Johnny said. "L.A. is the big time." He slid his machete into its sheath.

"Who cares?" Tess yawned.

"What a dork," Johnny stated, shaking his head.

They waited in silence until Grandpa returned bearing a huge metal pot and a large marble square.

"What's this?" Johnny asked, reaching out and tapping the marble.

"They used it to chop vegetables on, and they placed hot pans on it to prevent the kitchen counter from being scorched," Grandpa detailed.

"We could use one of those," Tess remarked.

"I'll take it with us," Grandpa said. "It will make a dandy gift for Betty."

"What are you doing with it?" Johnny wanted to know.

"Watch." Grandpa moved to the center of the bedroom and deposited the marble square on the floor, then positioned the pot on the marble. He went into another bedroom across the hall and came back with an armful of furniture fragments.

"We're going to use it for our fire!" Johnny deduced.

Grandpa nodded. He knelt and dropped the wood into the pot, then took a box of matches from his left front pocket. A minute later, a small fire was radiating light and heat about the room.

"Neat!" Johnny said. "I'll have to remember this trick."

"It's no trick," Grandpa corrected him. "They did it all the time before the war."

Tess unslung the brown leather pouch she wore draped over her left shoulder by a thin strap. "Can we eat now?"

Grandpa nodded, kneeling next to the pot.

Johnny crossed to the only window in the room and examined a network of cracks in the glass. "I can't believe this is in one piece!"

Tess opened her pouch and extracted three strips of beef jerky. "Here you go." She handed one to Grandpa and tossed a strip to her brother.

"So what's an amusement park?" Johnny queried, then bit into the tangy jerky.

Grandpa held his wrinkled hands over the fire. "An amusement park was where they went to have fun."

"Have fun?" Johnny said. "They had a special place for havin' fun?"

Grandpa grinned. "They had lots of places. Amusement parks, circuses, zoos, and others. I understand they have a few animals left at the zoo in Los Angeles. We'll visit it, if you want."

"I'd love to see it!" Johnny declared.

"I know of only one zoo left, the one in L.A.," Grandpa stated. "But amusement parks and circuses are things of the past. They died with the war. People had more important priorities, like merely staying alive. California had it pretty easy, compared to the rest of the country. But even here there were the looters, the Raiders, the mutants, and assorted killers."

"You still haven't told me what an amusement park is," Johnny observed, his mouth full of jerky.

"They were filled with rides of all kinds, tiny cars and trains and boats and . . ." Grandpa paused, pondering. "Roller coasters."

"What's a roller coaster?" Johnny asked.

"I don't really know," Grandpa said. "I've never been to an amusement park. Like I said, my father told me about them fifty years ago, and he learned about them from his father. You've got to remember it's been one hundred and five years since the war." He sighed. "My age must be showing. I don't recall details like I once did."

"You do fine," Johnny mentioned affectionately. "I hope I'm in as good a shape as you are when I'm your age."

"Thanks," Grandpa said, smirking. "I think."

"You know," Tess interjected, "sometimes I wish there had never been a war. I think we would be better off if those assholes hadn't decided to blow up the world."

"They didn't blow up the world," Grandpa stated, "but they came awful close."

"Do you think there will be another big war?" Tess inquired.

"World War Four?"

"Yeah," Tess said.

Grandpa shrugged. "There might be. As far as I know, we don't have any major countries left in the world. None of what they used to call superpowers."

"What's a superpower?" Johnny questioned.

"A country with people egotistical enough to believe they were super, and with enough military power to destroy their enemies ten times over," Grandpa replied.

"Were there a lot of these superpowers?" Tess asked.

"A few," Grandpa responded. "And I don't believe there will be another world war until superpowers are formed again."

"Why's that?" Johnny asked, delighting, as always, in his grandfather's entertaining explanations.

"I have this theory," Grandpa said. "World wars are caused by countries getting too big for their britches. A superpower is a war waiting to happen. So long as we have individual countries or nations trying to be on top, to control everybody else, we'll have world wars."

"We'll have wars forever," Tess commented.

"Maybe not," Grandpa said. "Not if we could set up a global government."

"A what?" Johnny said.

"A government of all the people on the planet," Grandpa stated. "It could be set up like this country used to be. There were fifty states before the war, and they lived in peace because they were presided over by a central government. Well, it could work on a global scale, too. We could have all the nations, or what's left of them, agree to create a world government."

"You're dreaming," Tess said.

Johnny looked out the window. "You sure come up with some weird ideas."

Grandpa stared at his grandson. "You don't think it would work?"

"How should I know?" Johnny responded. "All I know about government is that I don't like anyone tellin' me what to do."

"The Free State of California isn't a dictatorship," Grandpa remarked.

"Oh, yeah?" Johnny retorted. "Then what's this I hear about them making every kid go to school for five years, whether they want to go or not?" He frowned. "I'm glad I'm too old to go."

Grandpa laughed. "Before the war everyone attended school for at least twelve years."

"What?" Johnny said in surprise.

"That's right," Grandpa affirmed. "The school system,

like almost everything else, fell apart after the war. They didn't have enough teachers, and there was no way to keep all the school buses running." He paused. "Besides, the state government was too busy trying to restore order and maintain control. They didn't get the schools operating again in Los Angeles and the other big cities until about forty years ago, and it's been a slow process for them to organize schools in the smaller towns and rural communities."

"Well, I don't think they should have the right to force you to go to school," Johnny stated emphatically.

"I agree," Grandpa concurred, grinning.

"You do?" Johnny asked.

"Certainly," Grandpa said. "If you want to be dumb all your life, that's your prerogative."

"My what?" Johnny queried.

"I rest my case," Grandpa said.

"I don't need school," Johnny declared. "I learn everything I need from you, just like you learned from your dad."

"I'm afraid it's not the same," Grandpa disagreed.

Johnny, hoping to change the subject, gazed out the window. "It sure is dark out there."

"See anything?" Tess inquired.

"Only a mutant," Johnny answered.

Tess glanced up in alarm. "A mutant!"

"Yep. A giant rabbit breakin' branches from the trees," Johnny said, and cackled.

"You're not funny," Tess told him.

"Will you relax?" Johnny advised her. "There's nothin' out there to worry about."

The window suddenly exploded inward, showering shards of glass over the floor. Johnny was flung backwards, his arms flailing, and tripped over a chair, crashing onto his back.

"Johnny!" Tess screamed.

Grandpa drew his revolver, aiming the gun at the shattered window. The wind tore into the room, stirring the dust.

"Johnny!" Tess leaped to her brother's side. "Johnny!"

There was a ragged cavity spurting blood and brains in Johnny's forehead above his right eye. A pool of crimson was spreading around his head, soaking his hair. His mouth was twisted in a cockeyed grin.

"No!" Tess wailed.

Grandpa scrambled over to his granddaughter and grabbed her right wrist. "Tess! Tess!"

Tess was gawking at her brother, her eyes wide and frightened, her breathing loud and irregular.

"Tess!" Grandpa shook her. "Listen to me! We've got to get out of here!"

"But Johnny!" Tess cried.

Grandpa glanced down, frowning. "We can't do anything for him. And we can't stay in this house. Whoever did this has us hemmed in here. We've got to get out in the open where we can maneuver."

"I can't leave Johnny!" Tess protested.

"You must!" Garndpa hauled Tess to her feet and pulled her toward the doorway.

"No!" Tess objected, digging in her heels.

"Get a grip on yourself!" Grandpa snapped. "Come on, girl! You can do it! I don't want anything to happen to you too!"

They moved to the top of the stairs and Grandpa paused, listening.

"Johnny is dead!" Tess said softly, sniffling.

"Quiet!" Grandpa ordered. The lower level was quiet, seemingly safe. His grip on Tess tightened and he started down the stairs. One of the wooden steps creaked and he froze, waiting with baited breath, but nothing happened. He wondered how many enemies were lurking outside. If there was only one, he stood a chance of escaping with Tess. But there were few solitary Raiders abroad in the countryside. Most of the slime traveled in gangs, and usually they roamed the less-inhabited areas and retreated into the mountains if Free State soliders went after them.

The ground floor was plunged in inky blackness.

Grandpa stopped at the foot of the stairs, surveying the front door and the porch beyond. The door was suspended to the right of the doorway, and two strides past the door was the collapsed section of the porch. "We're going out.

Are you ready?" he whispered.

"I'm ready," Tess responded gamely.

"Good girl. Stay with me," Granda advised. He released her right wrist and crouched, then darted to the left side of the doorway.

Tess was right behind him.

Grandpa leaned against the jamb and peered outside, the cool air tingling his skin. He found himself wondering about the weapon used on poor Johnny. What could kill so silently? He had not heard a gunshot, not even the muffled retort of a firearm firing from a distance. And the weapon couldn't have been a bow, because there had been no arrow.

"Grandpa?" Tess whispered.

"What?" He looked at her.

"Why don't we stay in here until morning?" Tess inquired, her tone strained.

"Because if there's more than one out there," Grandpa said, "and if they decide to come in after us, we'll be trapped like sitting ducks."

"I wish I'd never bugged you about taking a shortcut," Tess remarked.

"Forget about that."

"Johnny would be alive right now if it wasn't for me!" Tess lamented.

"Tess, you've got to put Johnny from your mind for the time being," Grandpa instructed. "You need to concentrate on what we're doing. We have to make it into the trees on the far side of the road. We'll find a place to hide until daylight."

"I'll be okay," Tess said unconvincingly.

"And if something happens to me," Grandpa stated, "get to Los Angeles and find my sister. Betty will take you in."

"We never should have left the farm," Tess mentioned.

"Concentrate," Grandpa said. He slowly eased around the jamb to the porch, the Astra cocked in his right hand. The yard was a jumble of shadowy vegetation. He led Tess to the left, past the hole in the porch. They slid over the edge into a patch of waist-high weeds, ducking below the tops of the plants. Stooped over, they started toward the road.

Tess followed in her grandfather's footsteps, prudently endeavoring to tread as lightly as possible. She cast apprehensive glances at the murky woods, deathly afraid they were being watched by hostile eyes.

An owl hooted off to the north.

Another owl answered to the west.

Tess nearly collided with her grandfather when he abruptly halted. She saw him stare to the north, then the west, and suddenly he was sprinting to the east, toward the road. Tess took off after him, startled by his unexpected haste, dreading he had seen something behind her.

Grandpa reached the road and paused, looking over his left shoulder to verify Tess was still with him.

There was a pronounced swishing noise and a sharp thump, and Tess saw her grandfather hurled from his feet, his head jerking back, and her face was splattered with a spray of liquid. He was slammed onto his back by an invisible force. Heedless of her safety, Tess was next to him in one bound, kneeling alongside him and clutching his right shoulder. "Grandpa?" She leaned closer, and that was when she spied the fleshy hollow where once his right cheek and eye had been.

A third owl was hooting, this one to the south.

Tess, petrified, bolted, fleeing mindlessly to the east, into the forest on the far side of the road, exactly as her grandfather had directed. Branches tore at her clothing, impeding her progress, lashing her skin. She sobbed hysterically, unable to control her seething emotions.

A bulky shape rose in her path.

Tess shrieked in terror. A hard object clubbed her on the left side of her head, and she collapsed onto the dank earth, overcome by dizziness. She struggled to stand, but couldn't.

"What do we do with her, mate?" a gruff voice asked.

"Can we have some fun and games?" inquired someone else in a falsetto tone.

Tess became aware of figures looming above her. She raised her head, counting four of them.

"No fun and games," stated the tallest of the figures.

"Why not?" responded the man with the unnaturally high-pitched voice. "What can it hurt?"

"Yeah, guv! I could fancy a bit of the fluff," commented the one with the gruff manner.

"Are you disputing my leadership?" demanded the tallest figure.

The other two men simultaneously answered with a prompt "No!"

Tess rose to her elbows. She sensed the two men were wary of provoking the tall figure.

"No distractions until the job is done," the tall one said imperiously. "You knew my requirements before you signed up."

"I was just, you know, wondering," the man with the high voice mentioned obsequiously.

"You can stop wondering," the tall one said.

Tess was perplexed by their apparent lack of interest in her. Not one of them had acknowledged her presence.

"Nightshade," the tall one commanded.

Tess saw the fourth figure, the silent one, lift his arms and point something at her. She realized she was about to suffer the same fate as her brother and grandfather, and she opened her mouth to scream, to vent her shock and dismay.

The cool air was rent by a loud, inarticulate screech, a cry abruptly curtailed, fading to an odd gurgling whine and expiring as a gagging cough.

Unperturbed, the forest resumed its nocturnal pattern.

Prologue 2

"Do you think I've done the right thing?"

"I'm not paid to think, sir. Just to follow your orders."

The first speaker gazed out the window of his office in the Capitol Building at the twinkling lights of Denver, his blue eyes narrowed in thought. He ran his right hand through his clipped black hair and sighed. "Innocent lives could be lost if I've made a mistake."

"No one ever said being President of the Civilized Zone would be easy," commented the second occupant of the room, a man with rugged features, attired in a military uniform. His dark hair was cut short in the typical Army fashion. He studied the outline of his superior, noticing a slump to the shoulders covered by the blue suit, his brown eyes reflecting his concern.

"You're the commander of our armed forces, General Reese," the man at the window said. "And you're my most trusted confidant. I need your assessment of the situation."

General Reese shifted in his chair. He was seated in front of the President's desk, a manila file in his lap. "I don't see where my input can help any, President Toland."

President Toland, his hands clasped behind his back, glanced over his right shoulder. The window was situated to the rear of his oaken desk, and his standing position afforded him a clear view of General Reese's worried countenance. "Humor me, Barney," he said, grinning.

General Reese tapped on the manila file. "Okay. I think you're doing the right thing."

President Toland chuckled. "I'm not letting you off the hook that easy. Go over it again."

"We've been over it a dozen times already," General Reese noted.

"Then once more won't hurt, will it?" President Toland responded. He stared out the window at the panoramic view of Denver and the snow-capped peaks of the Rocky Mountains dimly visible on the western horizon despite the absence of the moon.

"No, sir," General Reese said.

"Then proceed," President Toland directed.

"We know we have a spy in our midst," General Reese began. "We know because the Family alerted us after they interrogated a captured Russian. What we don't know is the identity of the spy, but we suspect it is someone in a prominent position in our government. It could be one of your advisors."

President Toland sighed wearily. "One of my closest friends could be a traitor."

"We don't know that, sir," General Reese remarked.

"What?"

"We don't know if this spy is a traitor," General Reese elaborated. "By that, I mean we don't know if it's someone born in the Civilized Zone or someone the Soviets planted here."

"There's small consolation for me if it's a plant," President Toland said. "It's still someone I've placed my trust in, someone I've appointed to a high post. The blame is mine."

"Don't be so hard on yourself," General Reese advised. "Who could have anticipated the Russians using a spy?"

"*We* should have anticipated such an eventuality," President Toland replied. "We know the Soviets occupied a section of the eastern United States during World War Three, a corridor running from the Mississippi to the Atlantic Ocean, sort of a belt separating the Deep South from New York and the New England states. And we know the Russians want to dominate the entire country, or what's left of it. They'll stop at nothing to achieve their goals. So we should have expected dirty tricks on their part." He paused, looking at the far-off mountains. "And the Soviets aren't the only enemies we have. There are the Technics in Chicago, and Androxia in south Texas. Both of these city-states are actively attempting to extend their domination, to conquer the continent, if not the world, according to the information relayed by the Family. We owe Blade and Plato a debt of gratitude."

"Don't forget we have some friends out there too," General Reese stated. "There are the Flathead Indians in Montana, as well as the Cavalry, the horsemen of the plains, in the Dakota territory. We have the Moles in their underground city in northern Minnesota, and we have as allies the Clan, the refugees from the Twin Cities now living in Halma, about sixty or seventy miles west of the Moles. And last, but most importantly, we have the Family. We're not alone, sir."

"I know," President Toland said. "And it was wise of us to form the Freedom Federation, to sign treaties pledging to work together to restore some semblance of sanity to this land and to oppose our mutual adversaries." He stared at Reese. "But now I may have jeopardized the Freedom Federation by endangering its leadership."

"It's a calculated risk," General Reese admitted. "But it's the only way to flush out the spy."

"I hope so," President Toland declared.

"You should look at the bright side," General Reese suggested.

"How so?"

"You should be thankful we're still around to resist the Soviets, the Technics, and the Androxians. We're all that's left of the United States of America. Think of it. Once there were fifty states, and the U.S. was one of the largest countries in the world. Now all we have are Colorado, Kansas, Nebraska, Wyoming, New Mexico, Oklahoma, parts of Arizona, and the northern half of Texas. Denver is our capital. And although America has been renamed, although we call ourselves the Civilized Zone, we're as dedicated to maintaining liberty and safeguarding our freedom as the U.S. ever was."

President Toland leaned his forehead on the pane of glass. "And I believe my decision to invite the Free State of California to join the Freedom Federation was a logical result of that dedication. The more members the Freedom Federation has, the stronger we'll be, and the stronger we are, the less likelihood there is of our being defeated by the Russians or anyone else."

"So why are you agonizing over your decision?" General Reese asked.

President Toland returned to his desk and sank into his comfortable leather-covered chair. "Because to agree to holding the summit meeting in California is one thing," he responded with an air of self-reproach, "but to set up the leaders of the Freedom Federation as unsuspecting targets on the mere hope we can flush out the Russian spy is quite another. If one of the leaders is killed, I must assume full responsibility."

"Why don't you tell the other leaders about the spy?" General Reese proposed.

"I can't."

"Why not?" General Reese queried.

"What if the Russians have spies planted with the other members of the Freedom Federation? The more people we inform, the greater the risk of a leak," President Toland stated.

"Are you going to let at least Plato know?" General Reese questioned.

"I don't know," President Toland replied.

"You know you can trust Plato," General Reese asserted. "And if you don't tell him, at least inform Blade. You know damn well Blade isn't a spy. None of the Warriors are, for that matter."

President Toland grinned. "Ironic, isn't it? The ones I can trust the most are the Family's Warriors, not my own military personnel. Except for yourself, of course."

"Thanks." General Reese smiled. "Say. That reminds me. Where is this summit meeting in California going to be held?"

"A city called Anaheim, about twenty-seven miles from L.A."

Chapter One

The gleaming VTOL swooped down toward the airport from the northeast, its twin engines roaring. Dozens of aircraft of varying sizes were parked near their respective targets or taxiing toward one of the runways. Most of the planes preparing to take off were small, single-engine craft. The VTOL's speed decreased as it descended, and the aircraft angled in the direction of a terminal exclusively reserved for military use. A large crowd had gathered outside the terminal entrance to welcome the occupants of the VTOL. The craft reached a point 35 yards from the crowd and hovered. Moments later, accompanied by a muted whine, the VTOL landed. Two individuals detached themselves from the welcoming committee and walked toward the aircraft.

A door on the side of the VTOL opened as a ground crew pushed a portable flight of metal stairs up to the doorway. A lean, gray-haired man in a green Army uniform emerged from the VTOL. He smiled and waved at the man and woman approaching the craft. As he was going down the stairs, three more men stepped from the VTOL and paused at the top of the stairs to survey the huge airport in undisguised awe.

One of the trio was a veritable giant, standing seven feet in height and muscled like a latter-day Hercules. His black leather vest, green fatigue pants, and black leather boots seemed unable to contain his bulging sinews. A shock of dark hair hung above his probing gray eyes. Attached to his brown belt over each hip was a Bowie knife in a leather scabbard.

The second man was six feet tall, and while he lacked his companion's massive physique, there wasn't an ounce of fat on his wiry form. His long hair and handlebar moustache were both blond, his eyes blue. Buckskins clothed his frame, and moccasins covered his feet. Strapped around his slim waist were a matched pair of pearl-handled Colt Python revolvers.

The third member of the threesome was an elderly man with shoulder-length gray hair and a flowing gray beard. His blue eyes scanned the terminal and the crowd, and he noted the advancing duo. With the temperature in the low 70s and bright sunshine, his heavy flannel shirt, patched at the elbows, and his faded corduroy pants felt uncomfortably warm.

"Will you look at all this, pard!" the man in the buckskins said to the giant, marveling at the hustle and bustle of the airport.

"It certainly is the busiest airport I've ever seen," the giant conceded.

"And considering the extent of your travels," chimed in the elderly one, "that says a lot."

"We haven't seen all that much, Plato," commented the man with the Pythons.

"Really, Hickok?" Plato responded.

"We've seen a lot of Minnesota," Hickok stated, "and some of the Civilized Zone. I've been to Washington, D.C., and Chicago, or Technic City as they now call it. And Blade here has seen St. Louis, New York City, and Philadelphia." He paused, smirking. "Then again, I reckon we have seen a sizeable chunk of landscape."

"I'd say so," Plato agreed.

"We'd better join General Owens," Blade said, and together they walked down the stairs to the tarmac and the waiting officer.

Hickok gazed up at the aircraft. "I can't believe we got here so fast." He glanced at the gray-haired general. "What'd you call this contraption again?"

"A VTOL," General Owens answered, grinning.

"What do those letters mean?" Hickok inquired.

"VTOL stands for vertical take off and landing," General Owens explained. "It describes the capabilities of the aircraft."

"All those fancy words just means this buggy can fly like a jet, but it can take off and land sort of like a helicopter, right?" Hickok said.

General Owens nodded. "You've described it precisely."

"Too bad we don't have one of these at the Home," Hickok observed. "They'd come in right handy."

General Owens looked at the VTOL. "We could use more of these. We only have two still in service. They use less fuel than a conventional jet, and fuel is a precious commodity."

"There has been a chronic shortage of fuel since World War Three," Plato mentioned. "You are fortunate in one respect. The Free State of California has several operational refineries."

California has been very lucky," General Owens agreed. "The state sustained only two nuclear strikes during the war. San Diego was obliterated, and March Air Force Base at San Bernardino was hit. San Diego is south of here and San Bernardino is to the east, so the prevailing winds blew the fallout away from Los Angeles." He paused. "Frankly, I'll never understand why the Russians didn't toss more warheads at California. The state had over two dozen primary and secondary targets when the war began, not to mention all of the tertiary sites."

Plato thoughtfully scratched his head. "Only two nuclear strikes? I take it, then, your mutant problem has been minimal."

General Owens made a snorting sound. "I wish! Enough radiation polluted the environment to drastically affect genetic transmission, although the damn mutants didn't appear in any numbers until about a decade after the war. They reproduced at a fantastic rate, and the rural areas of California were practically overrun before the Army brought the mutants under control."

"You've eradicated the mutants?" Plato asked skeptically.

General Owens shook his head. "No, damn it! We've tried, but it's impossible. We have managed to clear them away from the urban centers and the smaller towns and communities. But it's not safe to travel in some parts of the state, particularly the mountains, unless you're well armed and with others."

"The mutants are everywhere," Plato noted. "I'm of

the opinion we will never rid ourselves of the genetic deviates. The mutant population will serve as an ever-present reminder of humankind's ultimate folly."

"Or putting it in basic English," Hickok quipped, "once a bunch of dummies, always a bunch of dummies."

"Speak for yourself," Blade said to the gunman.

"I knew it was too good to be true," Hickok cracked.

"What?" Plato inquired.

"Since we left Geronimo at the Home," Hickok said, "I figured nobody would be gettin' on my case this trip."

Plato looked at Blade and winked, then glanced at the gunman. "Unfortunately, Nathan, you invite ridicule by your outlandish behavior."

"What outlandish behavior, old-timer?" Hickok countered.

"Do you really want me to enumerate your bizarre traits?" Plato asked in feigned surprise.

"Name one," Hickok said.

Plato extended his right forefinger. "For starters, there's your peculiar propensity for conversing in that strange Wild West idiom."

"So I'm a mite creative with my palaver," Hickok commented. "What's wrong with being creative?"

"Is that what you call it? Being creative?" Blade interjected.

"What would you call it?" Hickok demanded.

"Being a ding-a-ling," Blade said, straight-faced.

Hickok stared at General Owens. "I can't get no respect, I tell you. This is the way they treat me all the time. Except for my pardner Geronimo, and he treats me worse."

"We have company," Blade announced.

A hefty man in a brown suit, his congenial features uplifted in a broad smile, and a petite blonde in a green dress reached the stairs.

"I'm Governor Melnick," the man in the brown suit said, greeting them. He offered his right hand to Plato. "And you're Plato, the leader of the Family, correct?"

"I am," Plato confirmed, shaking Melnick's hand.

"I am honored to meet you, sir," Governor Melnick

said sincerely, his brown eyes conveying his pleasure. "Your legend precedes you."

"My legend?" Plato asked.

"The Family's Legend. The envoys President Toland sent to propose this summit meeting told us all about your Family," Governor Melnick revealed. "You are very highly regarded by the other members of the Freedom Federation, and I look forward to having you as a staunch ally."

"You've decided to join the Federation then?" Plato asked hopefully.

Governor Melnick nodded. "I won't be making the formal announcement until tomorrow at the summit meeting, but yes, we have decided to become a member of the Freedom Federation."

Plato smiled, genuinely delighted at the news. "President Toland and the other leaders will be pleased to learn of your decision." He paused. "Has President Toland arrived yet?"

"Not yet," Governor Melnick said. "He's due to arrive in about three hours. The other leaders are all here. They've been transported to the summit site in Anaheim."

Plato glanced at the VTOL. "I want to thank you for agreeing to fly all the Federation leaders to the summit. As you are aware, traveling overland is a hazardous venture."

"I know," General Melnick agreed. "But flying all of you to California was the least I could do after President Toland accepted my offer to hold the summit here. Once the treaty is signed, I intend to propose using our two VTOL's on a regular basis to shuttle passengers, convey communiques, and generally serve as a courier service for the Freedom Federation. What do you think of the idea?"

"It's highly commendable and quite generous of you," Plato replied. "Currently, our messages can take weeks to reach other Federation members because of the distances involved. The last of the Civilized Zone's jets was destroyed five years ago, and none of the other Federation members possess aircraft." He gazed around the airport. "How have you managed to keep so many of your craft airworthy?"

"By assigning them our highest priority," Governor Melnick divulged. "California has abundant natural resources, but our supply isn't unlimited. The Free State government rationed fuel during the war, and the rationing wasn't lifted until about two decades later. We produce sufficient fuel to meet our needs, but every gallon is strictly accounted for. Utilizing aircraft is the only sensible means of conducting government, military, and commercial business. You have to remember California is eight hundred miles in length. So we've deliberately concentrated on maintaining our aircraft. We still use cars and jeeps and trucks, but not on extended trips unless there's no other alternative."

"Your government made a wise decision," Plato remarked.

Hickok abruptly made a show of clearing his throat. "Ain't you honchos forgettin' your manners?"

"How rude of me," Governor Melnick said, offering his hand. "You must be Hickok." He looked at the gunman's Pythons as they shook hands. "I've heard about your exploits."

Hickok grinned. "I reckon I am a mite famous."

"And modest too," Blade chimed in. He shook hands with the governor. "I'm Blade."

"Pleased to meet you," Governor Melnick said. "I know about you too. You're the head of the Warriors, and you're responsible for safeguarding the Family's compound."

"Among other duties," Blade stated, thinking of his beloved wife, Jenny, and his young son, Gabriel, both two thousand miles away at the Home, the Family's survivalist compound located near Lake Bronson State Park in northern Minnesota.

Governor Melnick nodded toward the VTOL. "I would have liked to meet more of your Family, but the VTOL's can only carry a maximum of five passengers."

"Then why'd you bring just us three?" Hickok asked.

"Because although we've used our VTOL's to transport five passengers on short hauls, and although we've added extra fuel tanks for long-range flights, we've never actually flown them beyond California's borders," Governor

Melnick disclosed. "We've simply had nowhere to go. Until we were contacted by your Federation, we assumed, based on past experience, that we'd receive a hostile reception anywhere we landed. In addition, we couldn't be certain of obtaining fuel if, by some chance, the craft ran low. So to play it safe we've stayed within our borders. Until now. These flights to pick up the Federation leaders are test runs. Theoretically, one of our VTOL's could fly five people from your Home to L.A., but I didn't want to run the risk of endangering your lives if the aircraft became low on fuel. With only three passengers, though, I knew our VTOL could easily make the trip. Which is why only three representatives from each Federation member are being flown to the summit meeting."

"A prudent judgment," Plato commented.

Governor Melnick turned toward the blonde. "I'd like you to meet my wife, Sharon."

Sharon Melnick stepped forward, smiling, about to shake Plato's hand, when her forehead suddenly exploded outward, spraying blood and chunks of ragged flesh and grisly gore in a wide arc. Her body stiffened and she toppled forward.

"Sharon!" Governor Melnick cried, catching her in his arms.

The two Warriors were already in motion. Hickok crouched, his hands twin blurs as the Pythons cleared leather. Blade gripped Plato's shoulders and pulled the Family Leader to the tarmac.

General Owens moved to assist Governor Melnick, placing himself between the governor and the terminal as he tried to support Sharon Melnick. The right side of the general's face erupted in a crimson shower and he fell backwards.

The crowd near the terminal was shouting and screaming. A dozen men in green uniforms were sprinting toward the VTOL.

"Get down!" Hickok yelled, springing to the governor's side and rudely hauling Melnick to the ground. The gunman scanned the crowd and the terminal, seeking the sniper. "Where the blazes is the varmint?"

Blade, covering Plato with his own body, spotted a

solitary figure on the roof of the terminal. "Hickok! The roof!"

Hickok glanced up and was off like a shot, dodging and weaving to present a difficult target. He could see the sniper was wearing a military uniform and holding a weapon, but he couldn't distinguish the type of weapon. The thing didn't look like a gun, but he couldn't be sure. He was still 30 yards from the terminal when he saw the sniper take aim, and he knew Melnick and Plato were the likely quarry. The gunfighter reacted instinctively, firing on the run, each Python booming, going for the chest because the head was partly obscured.

Incredibly, the gunman apparently missed a vital organ. The sniper staggered backwards several paces, shaking his head vigorously, and then moved back to the rim of the roof. He hefted his weapon, as if indecisive about making another attempt.

Hickok poured on the speed.

The sniper dropped from sight.

Hickok reached the line of soldiers running toward the VTOL. Three of them had stopped and were staring at the terminal. "Follow me!" the gunman shouted. He heard them pounding after him.

The sniper had not reappeared.

Hickok didn't slacken his pace as he approached the crowd. "Move!" he bellowed, waving the Colts, and the welcoming committee immediately parted, men and women frantically darting to the right and the left. He found a pair of glass doors in his path, and he used the thumb and forefinger of his left hand to snatch at the metal handle on the left-hand door, wrenching the door open and throwing himself to the left and squatting.

The sniper was on the far side of the sparsely crowded modernistic terminal, standing in front of another set of glass doors, his weapon to his shoulder.

One of the three soldiers was coming through the entrance.

Hickok looked to his right, his mouth wide to voice a warning.

The soldier was struck in the chest, the impact flinging him backwards into the two troopers behind him.

The sniper spun and raced through the exit on the far side.

Fuming, Hickok was up and running across the terminal, furious at himself for having missed and blaming his failure for the death of the soldier. As he sped in pursuit of the sniper, he speculated on the type of weapon the assassin was using. He hadn't seen a flash or heard a shot. The mangy coyote could be employing a rifle fitted with a silencer, but the contours of the weapon did not resemble those of a rifle. So what the blazes was the sniper using?

Hickok barreled through the glass doors on the opposite side of the terminal, discovering a spacious parking lot filled with various vehicles. Unsuspecting pedestrians ambled to and fro, some heading for the terminal or other points, some walking toward their cars. A number of soldiers were threading their way across the parking lot.

Damn!

Hickok jogged into the maze of vehicles, surveying the parking lot, realizing the lot was surrounded by a chain-link fence. There was only one exit, a gate on the east side manned by a pair of guards. He made for the gate, studying every vehicle and pedestrian. Quite a few of the people he passed had heard the shots and were gazing at the terminal in transparent perplexity. Several noticed his Pythons and gave him a wide berth.

A jeep suddenly gunned its engine, coming around a row of vehicles to the left.

Hickok peered into the jeep, the glare of the sunlight on the windshield momentarily obscuring his vision. The jeep was about 20 yards away and would pass within 15 feet of his position. He took another step, squinting, and there the bastard was, hunched over the jeep's steering wheel.

Not this time!

The sniper must have realized he'd been spotted, because the jeep surged forward, accelerating rapidly.

Hickok covered the 15 feet to the aisle in a mad rush, halting directly in the path of the oncoming jeep. He saw the sniper glare at him, and the jeep swerved slightly as the driver bore down at 50 miles an hour.

The sniper's intent was obvious; he was trying to run

over the Warrior.

"Hey! What's going on?" a nearby pedestrian shouted.

Hickok fired from the hip, the Pythons held close to his waist. The Colts boomed and bucked, twice apiece, and the jeep's windshield shattered and caved in. The gunman had deliberately refrained from planting a slug in the sniper. Hickok had decided he wanted the assassin alive if possible.

But fate intervened.

Ducking his head to avert the flying glass, the sniper inadvertently tugged on the steering wheel, sending the jeep hurtling to the left at a row of parked vehicles.

Hickok, transfixed, watched as the sniper got his due.

The assassin looked up, perceiving his danger. He yanked on the steering wheel, striving to avoid the parked vehicles, but he was too late. The front of the jeep smashed into the rear of a parked troop transport, the fender and the grill buckling. Unable to keep his grip on the steering wheel, the sniper was propelled up and over. He sailed out the gaping windshield, a sharp spike of glass attached to the upper frame tearing his back open in the process. His head slammed into the truck's tailgate with a sickening crunch, and he collapsed onto the hood of the jeep.

Hickok could hear the jeep motor sputtering and rumbling as he hurried toward it. He had scant hope of finding the sniper alive.

The assassin unexpectedly rose to his knees, reeling, a torrent of blood pouring from a hole in his cranium. He was fumbling with his right pants pocket.

Hickok held his fire, knowing the sniper would be easy to take. He was ten feet from the jeep when the assassin's hand came into view holding a hand grenade.

The sniper was on the verge of unconsciousness, but he mustered the strength to pull the pin on the grenade.

Hickok threw himself backward, twisting in midair, but he was a foot from the asphalt when the grenade went off, the thundering blast sending fragments of metal, glass, and pulpy tissue in every direction. The concussion smacked into the gunman with tremendous force, flipping him, sending him tumbling across the parking lot to collide with a parked car, his body lanced by bone-jarring pain.

A spiraling column of smoke wafted skyward from the demolished jeep.

Hickok slowly stood, leaning on the car, staring at the flaming wreckage. The sniper had committed suicide! And only demented fanatics or seasoned professionals snuffed their own lives when a mission had failed. Hickok doubted the assassin had been a fanatic. He straightened, a twinge of discomfort in his lower back, realizing his Pythons were still in his hands. With a practiced flourish, he twirled the revolvers into their holsters. One thing was for certain, he told himself. The summit meeting promised to be more eventful than he'd anticipated.

Chapter Two

"I can't believe I missed," Hickok said gloomily, absently starring out the limousine window.

"No one hits the bull's-eye every time," Blade commented by way of consolation.

"I do," Hickok stated morosely.

The two Warriors and Plato were in a black limousine, speeding to the southeast on the Santa Ana Freeway. Traffic was light. Plato, seated in the middle of the rear seat, glanced at the Warriors. Blade was behind the driver, a sergeant; Hickok was on the passenger side.

"Don't be so hard on yourself, Nathan," Plato advised Hickok, using the name bestowed on the gunfighter by his parents. Hickok, like most of the Family members, had chosen to adopt a new name on his sixteenth birthday, and he had selected the name of an ancient gunman he admired. The Founder of the Family's compound, the man responsible for spending millions of dollars to have the retreat constructed prior to World War Three, the man responsible for designating the site as the Home and dubbing his followers the Family, had instituted a special ceremony for all Family members. Upon turning sixteen, they were encouraged to research the vast Family library and pick any historical name they desired as their very own. The Founder had hoped this practice would insure that his descendants never lost sight of their antecedents. Later, the Family Elders had decided that any book, not just historical works, could serve as a source for the Naming ceremony, and Family members were even permitted to choose a name of their own devising. Blade had selected a new name predicated on his affinity for knives, while Nathan had taken the name of his childhood hero, James Butler Hickok. Over the years the gunman had lived up to his name, repeatedly exhibiting an infallible marksmanship. All of these thoughts went through Plato's mind as he gazed at the sullen gunfighter.

"I must not be gettin' enough practice," Hickok said.

"You practice more than anyone I know," Blade remarked, instantly regretting his lack of tact when his friend frowned and sighed.

"Then I'm gettin' old," Hickok declared.

"Don't be ridiculous," Plato admonished. "You're only thirty."

Hickok studied his hands. "Then I must be losin' my touch. And if I can't hit what I aim at, then I ain't much use as a Warrior."

"This isn't like you," Blade said. "You'd better snap out of it before we reach Anaheim, because I need you in top form for the summit meeting."

"Top form?" Hickok responded, and snorted.

Plato elected to change the topic. "This limousine is truly luxurious. We're receiving the red-carpet treatment."

"A limo. An army escort. Governor Melnick is pulling out all the stops," Blade noted, his features saddening. "I feel sorry for Melnick. We should have stayed in L.A."

"Governor Melnick insisted we leave for Anaheim," Plato reminded him. "I believe he was afraid of another assassination attempt."

"I have to admire the man's fortitude," Blade commented. "He wants to conduct the summit as planned. If something happened to Jenny, I don't know if I could go on with business as usual."

"We've come too far to turn back now," Plato mentioned. "Months of meticulous arranging and negotiating have gone into the preparation for this summit. Melnick knows we can't cancel the meeting." He paused, pondering for a moment. "Why would someone want to kill Governor Melnick? Except for the Raiders and other misfits General Owens told us about on the flight here, there isn't any organized opposition to the Free State government."

"So far as we know," Blade said. "And we've had to rely on government officials for our information."

"Do you suspect they have lied to us?" Plato inquired.

"No," Blade replied. "And I don't think Melnick was

the only target."

"What?" Plato said. "Why?"

"Because the first shot was meant for you," Blade stated. "Don't you remember? Sharon Melnick was about to shake your hand, and she stepped between the terminal and you, probably just as the sniper fired."

"Coincidence," Plato opined.

"Why?" Blade queried.

"Because only Governor Melnick and a few of his trusted aides knew we were arriving today," Plato detailed. "I seriously doubt they would want me dead. What motive would they have?"

"I'm not saying Governor Melnick was behind the assassination attempt," Blade explained. "I saw how his wife's death affected him. He loved her, and he wouldn't have brought her near us if he knew a sniper was on the terminal roof."

"Then who could be behind it?" Plato questioned. "We don't have any enemies in California."

"None we know about," Blade corrected him.

"It's the summit," Hickok unexpectedly interrupted.

"Why do you say that?" Plato asked.

Hickok glanced at the Family Leader. "The bozo I went after was a real pro. He wore an army uniform so he could blend in at the terminal without arousin' suspicion. He used a sophisticated weapon of some kind. And he had his getaway planned, right down to committin' suicide if he was captured. The man was a pro," he reiterated. "It was a professional hit, and Melnick and you were the targets."

"I agree," Blade concurred. "Hickok's right. I think someone is trying to disrupt the summit, and what better way to wreck the meeting than by killing off the leaders of the Federation factions and California?"

Plato frowned. "If your deductions are accurate, we can expect more trouble."

"We'll keep on our toes," Blade vowed. "We're at a disadvantage, though, because there's just the two of us to protect you."

"All of the leaders will be in the same boat," Plato

observed. "We were each allowed to bring two security personnel or assistants, and no more."

"I'm sure Melnick will tighten security at the summit site," Blade said. "But if professionals are after the leaders, there's no way we can prevent them from making more attempts."

Plato gazed out the front window at the four jeeps escorting the limousine. He looked over his right shoulder, finding four more. Each jeep contained four Free State troopers. "I think we can relax until we reach Anaheim," he declared.

Plato was wrong.

The lead jeep was cresting a low hill, well in advance of the rest, when there was a stupendous explosion and the jeep was engulfed in a brilliant fireball.

The sergeant slammed on the brakes, and the limousine slewed to a stop slantwise across the highway.

"Out!" barked Blade, yanking on the handle and flinging the door open. He looped his right arm around Plato's waist and leaped, his steely leg muscles carrying both of them to the hard asphalt. They landed with Blade on the bottom, intentionally cushioning the brunt of the contact. He surged erect, bearing Plato with him, racing for a stand of trees at the side of the Freeway.

A second jeep was blown to smithereens.

Blade carried Plato the final few feet, reaching the first tree and dodging for cover in the shelter of its wide trunk. None too soon.

Another detonation enveloped the black limousine, and the strike was dead center. The limo split in half as it was catapulted into the air, enshrouded by a sheet of reddish-orange flame.

Blade felt the ground tremble under his boots, and the stand of trees was buffeted by a gust of hot wind. He heard a deafening crash and risked a peek around the trunk.

The limousine was destroyed, a contorted jumble of scorched metal and burning rubber.

The other jeeps had stopped, and the soldiers were scanning the surrounding countryside for the source of the blasts.

Hickok!

Blade stood and ran to the edge of the highway, heedless of the danger, searching in both directions for his friend. "Hickok?"

The limousine was crackling and snapping as it burned.

A square-jawed officer, a captain, rushed up to the Warrior. "Are you okay?"

"Where's Hickok?" Blade queried anxiously.

"What?"

"Where the hell is Hickok?" Blade snapped, moving closer to the limo, as close as the intense heat would allow.

"Didn't he get out?" the captain asked.

Blade was worried by the same thought. What if Hickok hadn't made it out of the limo? What if the gunman's glum disposition had slowed his reflexes? What if . . .

"What the heck is the matter with you, pard? You look like somebody walloped you in the dingus."

Blade whirled to the right, and there was the gunfighter, nonchalantly emerging from a swirl of whitish smoke, his thumbs hooked in his gunbelt. "Where were you? I thought you bought the farm!"

"Nope," Hickok responded. "I lit out the passenger-side door and bruised my shins takin' cover behind this big old rock."

Blade breathed a sigh of relief. "Any signs of who did it?"

"I didn't see hide nor hair of the rascals," Hickok said.

"There's no sign of them," the captain confirmed. "But at least they've stopped."

Blade glanced at the gunman. "Mortar, you think?"

"Yep," Hickok laconically replied. "Or somethin' similar."

"Well, that settles it," Blade stated brusquely.

"Settles what?" the captain inquired.

Blade stared into the officer's eyes. "From now on we do this my way."

"We what? I'm under orders—" the captain began.

Blade's right hand flicked out and grasped the front of the officer's shirt. "Until we reach Anaheim, you'll take your orders from me."

"From you?" the captain exclaimed, futilely trying to

pry the giant's fingers from his uniform. "Now just hold on!"

Blade's eyes narrowed and his tone lowered. "You'll do as I say or else!"

"Blade! Don't!" Plato came around Blade's left and placed a restraining hand on the giant's arm. "Release him."

Blade ignored the command. "I'm responsible for your safety, Plato. And nothing is going to happen to you on this trip, not while I'm alive. We're going to do this my way from now on!" He glared at the captain. "Any objections?"

The officer, clearly flustered, nodded. "I'm under orders to get you safely to Anaheim. I don't care how we do it."

Blade released the captain's shirt. "I can rely on your cooperation?"

"You've got it," the officer pledged. "I don't want any trouble."

Blade pointed at the limo. "We've already run into some trouble."

"So what do you want me to do?" the captain asked.

"Strip."

The captain did a double take. "What?"

"Are you hard of hearing?" Blade queried impatiently. "I want you to strip. Remove your uniform."

"You're crazy," the captain commented.

Blade folded his arms across his chest. "Were you at the airport earlier?"

"Yes, I was," the captain answered.

"Then you know this is the second assassination try so far," Blade said. "Odds are there will be more. They were after the limo this time, and they stopped because they nailed it. They probably believe they've killed Plato, but we can't take that for granted. They might hit us again before we reach Anaheim, and I want to discourage them from trying."

"How?"

"If these bastards don't see any sign of Plato, they might leave us alone," Blade speculated. "So I want you, or one of your men, to give Plato a uniform and a helmet.

If we dress him up as a soldier and tuck his hair under the helmet, we might get away with it."

The captain grinned. "That's an excellent suggestion. I've been assigned to the summit detail, so I brought my dress uniform along. It's with my gear. I'll get it." He started off, then paused and looked at Blade. "See? All you had to do was explain what you wanted. I'm here to help you." He walked off.

"You shouldn't have manhandled him," Plato said to Blade. "We mustn't antagonize these people. We want them for our friends."

Blade shrugged. "Couldn't be helped."

Plato gazed at the smoldering limousine. "This attack confirms your theory. The persons responsible are trying to terminate the summit."

"Or terminate the summit leaders," Blade amended.

Hickok was surveying the landscape. "You know, it's right pretty hereabouts." He glanced up at the sky. "But a mite too warm for my tastes."

"We should have worn lighter clothing," Plato remarked. "California has always been famous for its salubrious climate."

"I wish you'd stop usin' them highfalutin' words," Hickok said. "Half the time I don't know what the blazes you're talkin' about."

Plato grinned. "Nathan, you're not as dumb as you pretend to be."

"What makes you say that?" Hickok rejoined.

"You never request definitions for the words I employ," Plato noted.

Blade stretched, his huge muscles bulging. "I like this weather. Minnesota gets too cold in the winter for my taste. I wouldn't mind living here all year long."

"California's weather is not always this mild in January," Plato mentioned. "In fact, General Owens told me they were in a cold snap until yesterday."

"A cold snap is better than four months of lousy weather," Blade observed.

"Who are you tryin' to kid, pard?" Hickok quipped. "You like this weather because you can prance around half naked without gettin' goose bumps."

The captain returned carrying his dress uniform. "Here you go. I hope it fits." He handed the uniform to Plato.

"Just so whoever's after us can't identify him from a distance," Blade said.

"The ploy might succeed," Plato stated. "A helmet will hide my hair, but what about my beard?"

"Tuck it under your shirt," Blade directed. "If you keep your chin down, you'll pass as a soldier."

Plato walked to the stand of trees.

The captain nervously scanned the vegetation on both sides of the highway. "I'll be glad when we get going. I don't like being out in the open."

"You and me both," Blade agreed.

"I radioed in a report," the captain said. "They're sending a helicopter from L.A. to provide aerial cover."

"Has Governor Melnick ever been attacked before?" Blade asked.

"No," the captain replied. "Except for the damn Raiders and the mutants and such, we never have any trouble. California holds elections every four years, just like the state did before the war. If the people don't like a politician, all they have to do is vote him or her out of office."

"When was your last election?" Blade queried.

"November," the captain said.

"What's with Plato?" Hickok interjected.

Blade glanced toward the side of the road.

Plato was emerging from the trees, but he was only partially clothed, wearing his brown corduroy pants and holding the uniform shirt in his right hand, and he was walking *backwards*.

Blade stared at Plato's naked back, puzzled, and then he detected a slight movement beyond the Family Leader. He whipped his Bowies from their scabbards and charged forward, bearing a bit to the right for a clearer view, his intuition shrieking a warning, knowing what he would see, his stomach tightening in anticipation. He came around Plato's right side, and there it was, a repulsive monstrosity straight from a madman's nightmare.

A slavering mutant.

Chapter Three

Once, the deviate might have been a feral cat, but now it was a deformed, grotesque horror. Three feet tall at the shoulder, its streamlined body was covered with splotches of brownish-gray hair alternated with patches of wrinkled, dry skin. The oval ears were utterly devoid of hair, but the feline face was unnaturally bushy. Slanted green eyes were locked on its prey. Fangs protruded from its upper and lower lips, and spittle seeped from its mouth and over its chin. The legs were short and sturdy, and its tail was a mere stump.

Blade didn't hesitate. He leaped, interposing himself between Plato and the mutant.

The cat was in motion, having shifted its attention to the approaching giant. It attacked, launching itself toward the giant's throat.

Blade had a split second to react. If he dodged aside, the thing would be on Plato with its slashing claws and teeth. His only recourse was to stand his ground, and stand it he did, twisting his torso to narrowly evade the mutant's raking claws. He plunged his left Bowie up and in, the razor point easily slicing into the feline's throat, burying the knife to the hilt.

The enraged mutant, impaled in midair, thrashed and swiped at the giant human.

Blade felt an intense stinging sensation in his left wrist and knew the cat had drawn blood. He let go of his left Bowie, allowing the mutant to drop to the ground.

Spurting blood, the mutant landed on all fours, but its stance was wobbly and its green orbs were glazing.

Blade swept his right Bowie up, then down, ramming the knife into the feline's neck, into the spine at the junction with the head. There was a distinct snap as the right Bowie was imbedded in the mutant, Blade's exceptional strength driving the knife all the way in, slamming the feline to the tarmacadam. He held onto the hilt as the mutant convulsed wildly, then expired.

"Thank you," Plato said.

Blade slowly straightened, wiping perspiration from his forehead with the back of his right hand.

"Why do you always do things the hard way, pard?" Hickok asked, standing to Blade's left with his Pythons in his hands. "You should have given me a clear shot."

"I've never seen anyone take on a mutant with a knife before," commented the captain, joining them. He was gawking at the dead feline.

Hickok noted blood on Blade's left wrist. "Are you okay, pard?"

Blade raised his left forearm and studied the trio of gashes extending from his hand to the middle of his forearm. Crimson coated his skin. "It's just a scratch," he remarked.

"You are lucky it wasn't one of the pus-covered ones," the captain said. "If a drop of that pus gets in your system, you're a goner."

"We call the pus-covered genetic deviates mutates," Plato mentioned, "to differentiate them from the typical mutants."

"Either one, you were lucky," the captain reiterated to Blade. "I have a first-aid kit in my jeep. I'll get some disinfectant."

"I don't need it," Blade said.

"We don't want you showing up at the summit with your arm all bloody," the captain stated. He hurried toward his jeep.

Blade knelt and yanked his Bowies from the mutant's body. He carried the knives to the edge of the highway and wiped the blades clean on a clump of tall grass.

Hickok, his Colts still in his hands, was alertly watching the vegetation.

Plato donned the uniform shirt. "Thank the Spirit the creature didn't attack before you intervened," he said to Blade.

The towering Warrior grinned at his mentor. "Weren't you the one who said this trip would be a—what were your words?—wonderful, scenic vacation?"

"I appear to have miscalculated," Plato remarked.

"If you want to finish gettin' dressed," Hickok offered. "I'll tag along to make sure nothin' bites you on the butt."

"Thank you." Plato and the gunman walked into the trees.

The captain hastened over with a bottle of hydrogen peroxide and a blue box of cotton swabs. "There's a roll of gauze in the first-aid kit I can use to bandage your arm after I get through applying the peroxide."

"I won't need a bandage," Blade said.

"Suit yourself," the captain acquiesced. "Let's go over here." He headed toward a jeep parked ten yards to the rear of the ravaged limousine.

"What's your name?" Blade asked as they passed the limo.

"Captain Di Nofrio, at your service."

"What's your first name?"

"Vincent," Di Nofrio said. "But you can call me Vinnie." They reached the jeep and he deposited the hydrogen peroxide and the cotton swabs on the hood. "Now let me tend your wound."

Blade held up his left forearm.

"So tell me," Di Nofrio said as he began to work on the gashes, "What's it like where you come from?"

"Cold."

"I mean your Home and all," Di Nofrio said, clarifying his query. "I've heard a lot about it, about your Family."

"What did you hear?" Blade inquired.

"I attended a briefing on the summit, on the different groups in the Freedom Federation," Di Nofrio explained. "You live in a thirty-acre walled compound in Minnesota, right?"

"Right," Blade confirmed.

"Why do you call the compound the Home? And why do you call yourselves the Family?" Di Nofrio queried.

"Kurt Carpenter, the man we call the Founder, the wealthy filmmaker who built the retreat just before the war broke out, was a very spiritual man, a moral man," Blade expounded. "He wanted his followers to live in peace together, to devote themselves to their close-knit group, to live like one big happy family."

"So Carpenter named his followers the Family," Di Nofrio deduced.

"Exactly. And to insure his followers and their descendants viewed the compound as theirs, and not just his, he—" Blade began.

"He called the compound the Home," Di Nofrio said, finishing the sentence.

"You've got it."

"We were also told about the Warriors," Di Nofrio mentioned. "You fifteen guys have quite a reputation."

"We have eighteen Warriors now," Blade divulged. "And three of them are women."

"Women Warriors?"

"What's wrong with having women as Warriors?" Blade asked. "You have female soldiers in the Free State Army."

"I know. It just never occurred to me you'd have women Warriors," Di Nofrio said.

"We also have three mutants," Blade disclosed.

Di Nofrio, in the act of dabbing the gashes with peroxide, stopped and glanced up in surprise. "Mutants?"

"Mutants," Blade confirmed. "The animals weren't the only species to experience mutations because of all the radiation and chemicals unleashed during World War Three. Human mutations are quite common in some areas."

"You have some of these human mutations at your Home?" Di Nofrio asked in stark amazement.

"Just the three Warriors," Blade elaborated. "And they weren't by-products of the war. They were created by a scientist, a genius in genetic engineering."

"Mutant Warriors," Di Nofrio declared, as if boggled by the concept.

"The arm?" Blade prompted.

"Oh." Captain Di Nofrio resumed his ministrations.

"Tell me about your borders," Blade stated.

"Our borders?"

"Yeah. California's borders. Do you patrol them? Are

sections fenced? How do you keep undesirable elements from entering the state?" Blade inquired.

"Oh. We use fences and patrols," Di Nofrio answered. "There are checkpoints on all the roads and highways."

"On every one?"

"Every one," Di Nofrio replied. "I was stationed in eastern California a few years ago, assigned to checkpoint duty. I was bored to tears."

"Little traffic, huh?"

"Are you kidding? There was no traffic," Di Nofrio mentioned. "No one in their right mind would want to leave California, so there's never any outgoing traffic. And incoming traffic is sparse. Except for California, the Civilized Zone, and a few other spots where there's some semblance of civilization, there aren't many cars and trucks in running order. So the few arrivals we do see have had to walk here. Those coming from the east must cross the Nevada desert, and I imagine most of them die before they reach our border." He paused. "Decades ago it was different. Right after the war, and until about forty or fifty years ago, there was incoming traffic on a regular basis."

"What about your northern border?" Blade questioned.

"We do have more incoming traffic from the north," Di Nofrio said. "But it's still not much compared to what it was years and years ago."

"Would it be easy for someone to sneak in?" Blade asked.

"Sure. We can't patrol everywhere at once, and it would be impossible to fence in the entire state. And there's always the Pacific Ocean. The Free State Navy, which is made up of old Coast Guard and U.S. Navy ships and boats, patrols our coastal waters, but it would be a breeze for a boat to land on any of our secluded beaches."

"So if professional assassins wanted to enter the state, they could practically do it in their sleep," Blade summarized, frowning.

"Do you really think these attacks were by professional hit men?" Di Nofrio inquired.

"Do you have a better explanation?" Blade rejoined.

"Nope. Guess not."

Blade heard footsteps and turned to find Plato and

Hickok approaching, Plato attired in a uniform with his beard tucked under the shirt. "You look spiffy," Blade joked. "Maybe you should enlist."

"Are we ready to depart? I'm eager to reach the summit site," Plato stated, addressing the captain.

"I'm done with Blade," Di Nofrio said. "But we should wait for the helicopter to arrive."

"The copter can catch up with us," Blade stated. "Let's leave now."

Di Nofrio shrugged. "Whatever you want."

"Looks like we're causin' quite a stir," Hickok remarked, pointing to the northwest.

Blade swiveled, espying a line of traffic blocking the Freeway several hundred yards distant. Three soldiers with M-16's were preventing the cars and trucks from proceeding.

"We can use this jeep," Di Nofrio proposed. He took off his helmet and handed it to Plato. "I'll be right back." He moved off, barking orders to his men, organizing the escort to depart.

Plato placed the helmet on his head, then carefully tucked his excess hair underneath. He looked at Blade. "One aspect of the attack on the limousine puzzles me."

"What aspect?"

Plato gazed at the wrecked vehicle. "Why didn't our assailants destroy the limousine first? Why did they destroy the two jeeps?"

"I can answer that," Hickok spoke up. "If those cow chips were usin' a mortar, they couldn't bank on hittin' our limo with their first shell. A movin' target is hard to hit with a mortar, even when you know the exact range. So they took out the jeeps, knowin' it'd slow us down or force us to stop, which it did. Once we stopped, we were easy pickings. Most likely, they had an approximate range on that low hill, but they didn't want to tip their hand by tryin' for our limo first."

"That's the way I see it," Blade agreed.

Hickok lifted his clenched left fist and commenced extending his fingers, one by one.

"What are you doing?" Blade asked.

"Countin' the days until I see my missus again," the

gunman replied. "The blamed summit is supposed to take three days. There are meetings today, a banquet tomorrow, another day of meetings, then the farewell shindig. So we won't fly to the Home until the fifth day."

Hickok sighed. "Pitiful."

"What is?" Blade queried.

"Havin' to put up with five days of this if we don't nail those buzzards sooner," Hickok said. "At the rate this trip is going, when we get back I'll need a vacation from my vacation."

Blade watched a flicker of orange flame sprout from the demolished limo, his facial contours tightening grimly, bothered by a somber thought.

If we get back!

Chapter Four

Governor Melnick had explained his reasons for selecting Anaheim as the summit site in a letter to the leaders of each Freedom Federation faction, a letter relayed by President Toland a month before the summit. Toland had initiated negotiations with the Free State of California by sending two envoys to the state under the protection of a Civilized Zone army convoy. Under explicit orders from Toland, the two envoys had remained in California for months, arranging the details of the summit. On their return to Denver with the good news, the envoys had carried the letters from Melnick.

Governor Melnick had picked Anaheim for several reasons. The state capital had been relocated from Sacramento to Los Angeles twelve years after World War Three. The rationing of fuel and the decline in the number of functional vehicles had made traveling to Sacramento increasingly difficult for the populace. Finding themselves relatively isolated from the major urban centers on the coast, the lawmakers and the governor had elected to move the seat of government. Because of Anaheim's proximity to L.A., and because one part of Anaheim, in particular, was ideally suited for the summit, Melnick had chosen the city as the site.

As with every other city in the state, Anaheim had suffered a drastic drop in population after the war. Six months prior to World War Three, close to 250,000 citizens had resided there. One hundred five years after the war, only 20,000 called Anaheim home, and the majority of them occupied the northern half of the city. The southern section was sparsely populated, and Governor Melnick had wanted a site where the summit would not attract undue attention, would not be surrounded by crowds of the curious every day. Melnick knew the leaders would require an undisturbed atmosphere for their discussions, and he picked the perfect spot.

Before the war, an elaborate amusement park, now fallen into decay, had drawn tourists by the millions to Anaheim. But while the park no longer resounded to the peal of laughter and the hubbub of excited voices, a hotel southwest of the park was periodically utilized for seminars, conferences, and other governmental functions. The hotel, Melnick had decided, was the ideal place for the summit.

Blade mentally reviewed the letter from Governor Melnick, which Plato had allowed him to read, as their Free State Army escort wheeled onto West Street. He saw the hotel ahead to the left, and off to the northeast was the dilapidated amusement park. The hotel and vicinity were literally crawling with soldiers, all of them carrying M-16's and holstered pistols.

"I'd like to see those assassins try something here," Captain Di Nofrio commented from behind the wheel. He steered the jeep toward the curb in front of the hotel.

Seated on the passenger side across from the officer, Blade frowned at the idea. "I wouldn't," he said.

"You don't have anything to worry about here," Di Nofrio assured the Warrior. "Our security is airtight."

"If there's one lesson I've learned from my years as a Warrior," Blade remarked, "it's never to become overconfident."

"Look at all the troopers we have here!" Di Nofrio stated. "How could the assassins possibly get past us to kill the leaders?"

"Where there's a will," Blade noted, "there's a way."

"Never happen," Di Nofrio said obstinately.

"I hope you're right," Blade mentioned.

"Do you have guards on the roof of the hotel?" Hickok asked from his seat behind the captain.

"Of course," Di Nofrio replied. "And there are guards posted at ten-foot intervals all around the perimeter. I'm telling you, if those sons of bitches get in here then I'll eat my shorts."

"Well-done or rare?" Hickok retorted.

"Never happen!" Di Nofrio reiterated.

Blade saw the helicopter hovering above the hotel. The whirly-bird had caught up with them about seven miles from Anaheim.

Captain Di Nofrio braked the jeep, then turned off the motor. He glanced over his right shoulder at Plato. The Family Leader was quietly sitting next to Hickok, serenely contemplating the activity around him. "The other Federation members are probably in the lobby," said the captain. "They've been socializing since their arrival, waiting for President Toland and yourself to arrive. They know you are due to arrive about this time."

"And there haven't been any attacks on the other leaders?" Blade thought to inquire.

"None," Di Nofrio said.

"No incidents of any kind?" Blade queried.

"There was one incident," Di Nofrio answered, the corners of his mouth turning downward.

"What incident?" Blade asked.

"One of the Cavalrymen caused quite a stir yesterday," Di Nofrio disclosed "The Cavalry leader, a Mr. Kilrane, brought two bodyguards with him. A Mr. Boone and a Mr. Hamlin."

"And?" Blade prompted.

"Well, Mr. Boone apparently took it upon himself to conduct some target practice without notifying security," Di Nofrio elaborated. "He took a half-dozen bottles from the bar and went into the gardens behind the hotel. You can imagine the commotion when he started shooting."

"Was anyone hurt?" Blade questioned.

"No, but some heated words were exchanged," Di Nofrio detailed. "A corporal made the mistake of referring to Mr. Boone as an ignorant clod . . ."

Hickok cackled.

". . . and Mr. Boone flattened the corporal," Di Nofrio concluded.

"That's Boone for you!" Hickok said. "I love it!"

"You know Mr. Boone?" Di Nofrio inquired.

"Sure do," Hickok said. "Kilrane, Boone, and Hamlin have been to our Home a number of times for Federation get-togethers. Boone has a rep as being fast with his irons, almost as fast as me." He paused, recollecting the fiasco at the airport. "Of course, he probably shoots straighter."

"What makes you say that?" Di Nofrio asked.

"Never mind."

"Let's go inside," Plato suggested. He removed the helmet and handed it to the captain, then extracted his beard from under his shirt.

"I'll go with you," Di Nofrio offered. "Governor Melnick has appointed an officer to act as your official liaison during your stay. I'll find him for you."

"You're not our liaison?" Blade queried.

"No. The liaisons are all high-ranking officers," Di Nofrio responded. "I believe a colonel has been assigned to you."

"Well, you find this colonel and tell him we already have our liaison," Blade instructed.

"You do? Who?" Di Nofrio asked, clearly confused.

"You," Blade told him.

"Me!" Di Nofrio exclaimed. "I'm not your liaison!"

"You are now," Blade stated.

Di Nofrio's brown eyes widened. "You can't be serious. I'm under orders to escort you here and then report to internal security. I expect to be assigned to oversee the guard detail on one of the hotel floors."

"Tell your superiors your assignment has been changed. I want you as our liaison," Blade directed.

"I don't know," Di Nofrio said, apparently flattered but unwilling to make waves.

"Give me one reason why we can't have you as our liaison?" Blade demanded.

"It's most irregular," Di Nofrio said.

"That's not a reason. Governor Melnick has gone out of his way to supply all our needs while we're here," Blade pointed out. "And he said if there was anything we wanted, anything at all, just say the word and it's ours." He paused. "I want you as our liaison. If your superiors want to know why, tell them I'm impressed by your professional behavior."

"You are?"

"Now why don't you go check in?" Blade advised. "We'll be in the lobby if you need us."

"Me? Liaison?" Di Nofrio climbed from the jeep, shaking his head in bewilderment. "I'll be right back," he promised and hurried off.

"Okay, pard. Clue me in," Hickok stated. "What's the real reason you want this tenderfoot as our liaison?"

"I'd relish learning your motive myself," Plato added.

"Di Nofrio is housebroken," Blade said.

Hickok chuckled.

Plato glanced from one Warrior to the other. "Would you elucidate?"

"What was the first thing your wife, Nadine, did with that puppy President Toland gave her last year for her birthday?" Blade asked.

Plato reflected for a moment. A grin creased his features. "She disciplined the canine whenever it urinated or attempted to defecate in our cabin."

"She taught it to behave," Blade said. "The dog is under her control, under her thumb so to speak. Well, Captain Di Nofrio is under our thumb. He won't give us any grief if we decide to deviate from the official program, and we might need the latitude if worse comes to worst." He smiled. "Besides, I like him. He reminds me of Nadine's puppy."

Plato stared at the hotel entrance. "Let's venture inside. I'm eager to visit with the other delegates."

Blade stepped from the jeep, admiring the structure. Because the government regularly used the hotel, the building was maintained in superb condition. The polished glass doors glistened in the sunlight.

Hickok stretched after clambering from the vehicle. "I hope they've got some grub in there. I'm starved."

Plato joined them, carrying his flannel shirt and corduroy pants bundled under his left arm. "Shall we?" He motioned toward the glass doors.

Blade walked up to the doors, nodded at a pair of guards standing at attention, and opened the right-hand door for Plato.

The Family Leader squared his sloping shoulders and marched inside.

Hickok halted, indicating Blade should enter next. "You're the chief Warrior. Protocol and all that."

Blade laughed, followed Plato. "What do you know about protocol?" he queried over his left shoulder.

"Enough to know I should wear my knee-high moccasins when dealin' with political types," Hickok answered. "Do you recollect our history lessons in the Family school? Back in the old days, before the Big Blast, the politicians were either feedin' the folks a load of bull or stealin' them blind."

"The Freedom Federation leaders aren't stealing their people blind," Blade remarked, "and they don't feed anyone a load of bull."

"Oh yeah?" Hickok rejoined. "Then why is it, every time I attend one of these summit shindigs and listen to all those long-winded speeches, I get a mite soggy from my knees down to my feet?"

"If you'd use a toilet or a tree you wouldn't have that problem," Blade quipped.

The hotel lobby was ornately furnished, with plush blue carpet, mahogany furniture, freshly painted walls, and potted plants in profusion. Packed from wall to wall with prominent and minor bureaucrats, military types, assorted gofers, and members of the hotel staff, the lobby was filled with the hubbub of dozens and dozens of intermingled voices.

Plato stopped, surveying the scene.

Blade stood alongside Plato's right arm, searching for the other members of the Freedom Federation. They were easy to spot, their attire causing them to stand out like the proverbial sore thumb.

Twenty feet off to the right were the representatives of the Cavalry, the horsemen of the northern Plains, a protective association controlling the former state of South Dakota, dedicated to defending the ranchers, farmers, Indians, townspeople, and other occupants of their territory. All three Cavalrymen were dressed in their usual garb: buckskins. Their leader, Kilrane, was a handsome man with blue eyes and streaks of gray in his brown hair. He was a big man, and he wore a Mitchell Single Action revolver on his right hip. With him were his two closest associates, Boone and Hamlin. Boone was tall and lean, over six feet, with broad shoulders and a narrow waist. His brown hair was worn shoulder-length. Buckled around his waist were a matching pair of 44 Magnum Hombre single-action revolvers. Hamlin was a small man with a scruffy beard and a wispy moustache. A Winchester was slung over his back.

Conversing with the Cavalrymen were the emissaries from the Clan. Hundreds of refugees from the Twin Cities had settled in a town called Halma, located six miles from the Family's compound, and named themselves the Clan in imitation of the Family. Zahner was their leader, a man of average height with sharp blue eyes, fine brown hair, and a distinctive cleft in the middle of his upper lip. He was wearing a brown shirt and brown trousers. To his right was one of his two lieutenants, a huge black man known as Bear. A curly Afro served to enhance Bear's impressive stature. He preferred to wear a fatigue jacket and fatigue pants. To Bear's right was Zahner's second lieutenant, a bearded man dressed all in black. Brother Timothy was the spiritual standard-bearer for the Clan.

Blade stared straight ahead. The three envoys from the Flathead Indians were talking to several bureaucrats. Conspicuous by her youth and her stately bearing, seventeen-year-old Star was the head of her tribe. Her father, the former Chief, had perished in battle. Largely because of her unflagging efforts to inspire and reunite her tribe after a military setback, she was later chosen to lead them. Her lovely black hair hung to her waist, partially covering her beautiful brown leather dress adorned with intricate beadwork. Attending her were her two counselors. Both were wearing their finest buckskins and robes. Red Cloud was the older of the counselors, in his forties, with a wisdom belying his years. Lone Bear was in his twenties, and Blade noticed his eyes seldom strayed from Star.

Seated by themselves in the rear of the lobby, aloof from the proceedings, were the three Moles, the representatives from the subterranean city called the Mound located in northern Minnesota. Their leader, Wolfe, ruled them with an iron hand. While not a despot, Wolfe came the closest of all the Freedom Federation leaders to being a true tyrant. He was exceptionally tall and abnormally thin, with an unruly mane of red hair crowning his haughty countenance and complementing his intense blue eyes. The color purple was his favorite, and he wore a purple shirt and purple slacks. He was flanked by two flunkies.

"I'd like to get their attention," Plato absently commented.

Hickok cupped his hands around his mouth and stepped forward. "Quiet!" he bellowed. "An hombre can't hear himself think with all you yahoos yackin' like a bunch of ninnies!"

Every eye in the lobby focused on the emissaries from the Family.

"You wanted their attention, you've got it," Hickok said to Plato.

There were cries of greeting from some of the Freedom Federation members, and the Cavalry, Flathead, and Clan representatives started forward.

Plato held up his right hand, grimly surveying the crowd, bringing all motion to a standstill. "My friends, it is a great pleasure to see all of you once again! But I'm afraid our reunion must be tempered by the tragedy at the airport."

Several of the Federation members exchanged confused glances.

Plato's forehead creased. "Weren't you informed?"

Zahner, the head of the Clan, spoke for the rest. "Informed about what?"

"About an hour and a half ago," Plato detailed, "there was an assassination attempt on Governor Melnick and myself at the airport. Governor Melnick's wife, Sharon, was slain."

Stunned expressions filled the lobby.

"Enroute to Anaheim we were attacked again," Plato continued. "Accordingly, I'm requesting an emergency session of the Freedom Federation Council to convene immediately. It is imperative we develop contingency plans and formulate a strategem to neutralize this threat to the summit."

Kilrane took several steps forward. "They have a conference room we can use."

"Then let's repair to the conference room and conduct our meeting," Plato suggested.

"I'll show you where it is," Kilrane offered.

Plato nodded and went to follow the Cavalry leader, but Blade grabbed his wrist.

"Hold it," Blade said. He released Plato and beckoned for the Federation members to gather around him.

Star came up to Plato and gave him a hug. "I wouldn't care if the world was coming to an end," she stated affectionately. "You still get a hug and a kiss from me." So saying, she pecked him on the right cheek.

"I'm overjoyed to see you again," Plato told her. During her twelfth year Star had resided at the Home, living with Plato and his wife, Nadine.

"Listen up," Blade addressed the clustered delegates. "I expect the Free State Army will post guards on the conference room doors, but we are not going to rely on them for our security. We must protect our leaders ourselves. We'll post our own guards to supplement the soldiers."

"That's a good idea," Kilrane remarked.

"Then we should pick one of us to serve as security chief for the Council," Blade recommended.

"That's easy enough," Kilrane stated. "You're more qualified than anyone else." He looked at the others. "Any objections to Blade being our security chief?"

No one objected.

"Okay, then," Blade said. "While Plato, Kilrane, Zahner, Star, and Wolfe conduct their meeting, I want to get together with the rest of you right outside the conference room." He glanced at Hickok. "All except for you."

"Me?" the gunman commented.

Blade looked at Boone. "And you. I understand you've taken a tour of the hotel grounds."

Boone grinned. "That's one way of putting it."

"I want Hickok and you to patrol outside the hotel," Blade directed. "Keep your eyes peeled for anything suspicious."

"Will do, pard," Hickok said.

"Where is this conference room?" Blade asked Kilrane.

The Cavalry leader pointed to the right. "Over there."

Blade looked up, scanning the right-hand side of the lobby, his gaze alighting on a solitary soldier standing at the very rear near an open door, a soldier with an M-16 pressed against his shoulder and aimed at the Federation delegates!

The sniper was leering as he sighted his M-16.

"Look out!" Blade shouted, diving, tackling Plato and bearing him to the carpet.

The lobby was rent by the metallic chatter of an automatic rifle. Screams and yells punctuated the gunfire.

Blade looked up in time to see one of Wolfe's flunkies take a shot in the head and topple over. The hapless man had been standing in a direct line between Plato and the assassin. Everyone else was flattening or ducking for cover behind furniture. With two notable exceptions.

Hickok and Boone had drawn and spun as the firing began, but lacking Blade's height, they were unable to catch a clear glimpse of the sniper until the firing had stopped. They saw the assassin dart through the open door at the rear of the lobby and took off in pursuit, Hickok glancing back to insure Blade and Plato were unhurt.

Blade leaped to his feet. The sniper had simply sprayed his rounds in the general direction of the Federation delegates, and he had mowed down ten Free State citizens in the bargain. Crimson puddles dotted the blue carpet while groans of anguish wafted to the ceiling. Blade was relieved to discover Wolfe's assistant was the only Federation casualty. "Let's get to the conference room! Now!" he ordered.

Plato slowly stood, scowling as he surveyed the littered bodies. Assistance was being rendered to the injured, while Wolfe was staring at his fallen flunkie with casual disinterest. "Most illogical," Plato remarked.

"What is?" Blade asked.

"This attack," Plato said. "We were the sniper's target, yet he indiscriminately slaughtered innocent bystanders on the slim chance of slaying us. Why didn't he bide his time until a more favorable opportunity arose?"

"Who knows?" Blade responded, shrugging. "They'd

already tried twice and failed. Maybe they're getting desperate. Or maybe this sniper was impatient or an amateur. Or maybe they just wanted to scare the other Federation delegates into calling off the summit." He scrutinized the lobby. "So much for Free State Army security! They should have warned the delegates about the airport attack."

"I'm positive Governor Melnick is too preoccupied at the moment over the untimely demise of his wife to have given any consideration to contacting the delegates. Then again, he may have surmised security here was adequate to counter any threat, and felt there was scant justification for alarming the Federation members." Plato looked at the dead Mole. "Hindsight is invariably perfect."

Blade saw Kilrane waiting for them ten yards away. "Let's get to the conference room," he advised.

"What about Nathan and Boone?" Plato inquired.

"They can take care of themselves," Blade replied.

From afar, from the rear of the hotel, sounded the booming of a revolver.

Chapter Five

Hickok and Boone reached the doorway through which the sniper had disappeared and paused, Hickok to the right of the door, Boone to the left, while they peered past the jamb. They found a corridor leading to the rear of the hotel, an empty corridor, and they cautiously jogged toward another door at the end of the passage, alert for any movement. They reached a closed door in the center of the corridor on the left side and halted.

Hickok, careful to keep his body to one side of the doorway, gripped the knob and tried to twist it, but the doorknob refused to budge. "Locked," he whispered.

"Do you think the son of a bitch is hiding in there?" Boone asked.

"I doubt it," Hickok responded. "If the varmint had any brains, he's skedaddlin' for the hills right about now. Come on." He raced to the far door, Boone on his left side.

The door was slightly ajar.

Hickok hesitated, his intuition blaring. There was a small window in the upper half of the door, and through the glass could be seen lush green vegetation. The gardens Captain Di Nofrio had mentioned. Hickok doubted the security people would leave an exit unlocked while the summit was in progress. Which meant the assassin must have picked the lock to gain entry, and had probably fled through the same door.

"What is it?" Boone queried.

"Stay back," Hickok warned. There was one way to tell if his supposition was correct. He backed up several paces, then charged the door, slamming his left shoulder against the wood, flinging the door wide and plunging to the right, landing on a swath of grass and rolling, coming up on his knees with his Pythons leveled even as the window in the door exploded in a tinkling shower of glass shards.

Why hadn't he heard a shot?

Hickok rose and raced to a large tree ten feet off, crouching with his back to the trunk. There should have been a shot! But what if the sniper had discarded the M-16 and was using one of those mystery weapons, the same kind as the joker at the airport? Those lethal beauties didn't make a sound. He peeked around the trunk, probing the profuse plant growth for the assassin.

Just then Boone sprang through the doorway, bearing to the left, making for a hedgerow 50 feet away.

The assassin suddenly appeared, preparing to fire, standing near a Bigleaf Maple twenty yards off, exposing only his eyes, nose, chin, and arms as he sighted on Boone.

Hickok's right Python blasted as he snapped off a shot, aiming for the sniper's left arm because only a narrow strip of the man's face was visible. The Warrior didn't want to take a chance on missing with Boone's life hanging in the balance, so he went for the largest observable part of the assassin's anatomy. Hickok always preferred a head shot, where feasible, but adapted as circumstances dictated. Whenever the Warriors discussed their techniques, Hickok inevitably advocated the head shot as the ideal target in a life-or-death situation. As he'd stressed time and again, a slug in an enemy's torso did not guarantee instant death; the foe might live long enough to get off a final, and potentially fatal, round. But a bullet to the brain, particularly if from a high-caliber firearm, usually snuffed an opponent on the spot. "No brain, no pain," was Hickok's motto. At the airport earlier he'd been forced to go for the chest because the sniper's face had been partially hidden by his weapon, and predictably the sniper had survived. Now, as he went for this new assassin's left arm, the Warrior was gratified to see the arm jerk to the right as the sniper grimaced and ducked from sight.

Boone reached the hedgerow in safety.

Hickok charged from cover, sprinting toward the Bigleaf Maple, weaving back and forth.

Boone raced after the Warrior, trying to catch up.

Hickok reached the tree and rushed around the trunk. Blotches of blood speckled the ground. He knew it! He'd hit the varmint! Hickok saw a trail of red spots leading from the Bigleaf Maple to a gravel-covered trail eight feet away. He was off in a flash, using the intermittent drops of blood as a guide, turning to the right on the gravel trail and almost tripping over a body sprawled in his path. The gunfighter glanced down, discovering a dead Free State soldier with his forehead blown out. He hurried on, sticking to the winding, circuitous trail, scarcely noticing the botanic wonders surrounding him. The footpath curved sharply to the left, and on the straight stretch beyond were four more deceased troopers.

The assassin sure was a deadly S.O.B.

The minutes dragged by, the frequency of the dots diminishing. Twice Hickok was compelled to backtrack after taking a fork in the trail and traveling 15 to 20 yards without finding a blot of blood. He chafed at the delays, knowing the sniper was getting away. His impatience overrode any inclination to wait for Boone.

A turn to the right revealed three additional victims, soldiers contorted in the throes of death, all three shot in the head with the mystery weapon. Hickok was stepping over one of the troopers when he paused, his blue eyes narrowing. The left side of the trooper's face was gone, and there was a small hole in the back of the man's helmet. Whatever had killed the soldier had penetrated his metal helmet and burst out the side of his face.

Or had it?

Hickok had seen the effects of dum-dum bullets on countless occasions; he used hollow-point bullets in his Pythons. But the damage caused by the assassin's weapon was far worse. The exit holes, if such they were, were larger, much larger. And it seemed as if the projectiles had exploded the faces of the assassin's victims *outward from within*.

What in the world could do such a thing?

Hickok continued his pursuit, the path bearing in a northeasternly direction. The gardens abruptly ended at a brick wall. Yet another dead trooper was lying at the base of the wall. The gunfighter looked in both directions, spying a red streak on the wall six feet to his right. The assassin had escaped!

What now?

Hickok's hesitation was fleeting. He could either return to the hotel and permit the scum to make a clean getaway, or he could stay after the skunk and hopefully nail him. Since Blade and Plato were all right, he wasn't needed at the summit. The way he saw it, some sightseeing was in order. He twirled the Colts in their holsters, crouched, and leaped, extending his arms and grasping the lip of the eight-foot wall. His shoulders straining, he pulled himself up until he was on his stomach on top of the wall, studying the terrain ahead.

A jumble of weeds, brush, and forest covered the countryside. A few tall, decayed structures were in sight to the northeast.

Hickok recalled seeing the same structures when their jeep had exited the Santa Ana Freeway to travel to the hotel. What had Captain Di Nofrio mentioned about the place? It was an old amusement park, and hadn't been in service since the war.

Maybe someone was using it now.

As he dropped to the ground, Hickok remembered Governor Melnick's letter to Plato. Blade had let him see the correspondence, and the invitation to the summit had briefly referred to the amusement park. Each of the leaders in the Freedom Federation had received a similar letter.

Whoa there! What were those!

Hickok knelt and examined a set of bootprints in the soft earth near the wall. Crimson spots circled the prints. He stood and jogged to the northeast. The assassin's bootprints were spaced close together, indicating he was walking, not running. The cow chip must think he's safe, and no one is after him. Hickok grinned. He couldn't wait to show the varmint how wrong the skunk was!

The tracks led in the direction of the abandoned park. They traversed a field, then entered a dense forest. Fortunately, once in the woods, the assassin stuck to a well-used animal run.

Hickok wanted to capture the assassin alive, if possible. There were too many unanswered questions for his liking. Why were the hit men trying to disrupt the summit? Where did they come from? And the biggie: Who had hired them?

He knew the Russians had planted a spy in the Civilized Zone, in President Toland's administration. Had the spy discovered the location of the summit? Were the Russians responsible for sending the hit squad? After his experiences with the Soviets in Washington, D.C., he wasn't about to put anything past the rascals. So immersed did he become in his speculation, that Hickok failed to perceive the weed-and vine-choked fence until he made an abrupt turn in the trail and nearly collided with it.

The fence was a chain-link affair, betraying evidence of rust where the links were exposed to the elements. A coat of vegetation cloaked the fence from the top to bottom.

What was that?

Hickok crouched, examining an opening in the vegetation at ground level. Someone had cut a large hole in the fence, then aligned the vines and weeds over the hole to hide it. But they'd neglected to cover the middle of the hole, and a shaft of sunlight was shining through the gap. Hickok dropped onto his stomach and slowly crawled to the other side. He carefully surveyed the dense undergrowth, on guard for an ambush, and only after he was satisfied the assassin was not lying in wait for him did he rise and resume his trek.

The vegetation on the inner side of the fence was of a different variety than the plant life outside. Ferns and moss covered the dank earth. There were fewer big trees, but a profuse mushrooming of slim trees packed closely together. One type was quite unusual.

Hickok paused to inspect a stand of the strange trees growing alongside the faint trail he was following. None of the trunks were any wider than his arms; the bark was exceptionally smooth and glossy; and the tree was segmentalized into distinct sections of equal length separated by thin ridges. He ran his fingers over the velvety bark, genuinely amazed. Never in all his travels had he seen such a peculiar tree. Reminding himself to ask Plato about it, he cautiously continued to the northeast.

There was no rush now.

Hickok was certain the assassin believed his escape had gone flawlessly. And if the hit man didn't think anyone was on his trail, he'd grow careless, less watchful. Which was exactly what Hickok wanted. If he could catch the assassin unawares, he stood a better chance of taking the bastard alive.

A patch of blue became visible ahead.

Hickok realized the trail was approaching a body of water and he became alarmed. What if the assassin had stashed a boat on the bank? He broke into a run, covering 50 more yards before he emerged from the forest on the shore of a small lake.

There was no sign of the assassin.

Hickok began circling, searching the shore for bootprints or drops of blood. He found a few tiny crimson drops and guessed his quarry was moving to the north around the lake. The Warrior followed suit, staying close to the water where he could make better time, loping along at a dogtrot.

An object appeared in the lake, a few hundred feet ahead and about 20 feet from shore.

The gunman slowed in case the object was a boat. After traversing a hundred feet or so, he discerned the thing in the water was indeed a boat, but a gutted, rusted wreck, an ancient craft that apparently sank decades before, perhaps even during the Big Blast. He jogged 30 more feet.

Somewhere a bird was chirping.

Hickok caught a glimpse of something tremendously huge skulking in the vegetation to his left. He drew and whirled, hoping he could get off a shot before whatever it was pounced. A grayish form was standing in the midst of a stand of the strange trees. He dove to cover behind a clump of weeds.

Nothing happened.

Hickok pursed his lips in perplexity and raised his head for a better view.

The thing was just standing there in the deep shadows.

What the blazes?

Hickok rose to his knees, striving to identify the alien creature, confused by its inactivity. Maybe the critter wasn't hostile. He stood, the short hairs on the nape of his neck tingling. The animal was gargantuan, and he assumed the thing was a mutant. What else grew so enormous?

The blasted brute was still just standing there.

Hickok edged toward the creature, his Colts cocked, his fingers on the trigger. If the beast charged, he figured he could always jump into the lake. Some animals weren't too partial to water except for drinking.

The wind stirred the peculiar trees, revealing a pair of whitish protuberances on the head of the critter.

His curiosity aroused, Hickok advanced to within eight feet of the bulky form. Details became clearer. He could see two colossal ears and a snake-like nose. The whitish projections were horns of some sort. No! Not horns! Tusks! Suddenly he perceived the creature's identity, and astonishment washed over him.

What the dickens was an elephant doing in southern California?

Hickok tentatively walked closer, attempting to remember what little he knew about pachyderms. If he showed he was friendly, maybe the elephant wouldn't attack. "Howdy, there, big fella," he greeted the jumbo animal. "Don't fret none. I ain't here to harm you."

The elephant was staring at the gunfighter with glassy brown eyes.

Was the critter sick? "Any more of your kind around here, big guy?" Hickok asked, hoping his talk would calm the beast. "Where'd you come from, anyway? I know they used to have critter prisons called zoos. Did your great, great grandpappy belong to a zoo hereabouts?"

The elephant wasn't budging, wasn't reacting in any way.

Hickok was only four feet from the pachyderm, and his brow furrowed in bewilderment. The elephant was filthy, caked with grime and dust, and its tusks displayed discolored patches of pale yellow. And the animal's eyes hadn't blinked once since he first saw it.

Was it dying?

Hickok peered upward at the trunk and head, trying to penetrate the shadows enshrouding its face. He holstered his left Python and gingerly reached overhead, tapping the trunk.

Hard as a rock.

"What the heck!" the gunfighter blurted. He gripped the trunk, astounded to discover the elephant was a fake. The creature was artificial, constructed of a plastic-like substance.

A bogus pachyderm?

Hickok holstered his right Colt and ran his fingers over one of the tusks. Why had someone built this mysterious marvel? Was the elephant part of the amusement park? He'd read about zoos and amusement parks and carnivals and such in the Family Library, the extensive collection of hundreds of thousands of volumes personally selected by the Family's Founder. During his early schooling years, the Elders had taught several courses dealing with the prewar society, one of which had briefly delved into the fanatical devotion to diversion exhibited by the so-called civilized nations. But who would have thought they'd go so far as to make a phony elephant? Why didn't they just exhibit the real thing? Maybe they were trying to save money on their feeding bill. Or more likely, they couldn't find anyone willing to spend all day following the elephant around with a shovel.

Hickok shrugged and headed to the north along the shore. Those prewar types sure were loco. He wondered if he would encounter any more artificial animals, and his question was answered 40 yards further on.

This one was an alligator, a whopper of a reptile at least ten feet in length, lying on the shore with the tip of its tail in the water.

Hickok admired the superb craftsmanship as he neared the fake gator. The detail work was magnificent. There was a broad, rounded snout, a thick, powerful body, and a wide tail. The body and the tail were capped with ridges of triangular spikes. Its well-armored skin was a light shade of black. The ancient artisans had even managed to duplicate the musculature. How splendid! The gator's protruding eyes were closed as if the reptile was at rest.

The gunman was ten feet from the alligator when he startled a big bullfrog squatting on the bank. The bullfrog leaped away from the human, inadvertently bounding toward the gator. One of its leaps carried the amphibian to within a foot of the reptile, and the bullfrog abruptly whirled and executed a tremendous vaulting arc into the water.

Hickok chuckled. Stupid frog! Scared of a dumb fake alligator! The gunman was four feet from the reptile when he noticed how clean it was. Being exposed, the construct was probably kept free of dirt by periodical rainfall.

Hickok elected to step over the reptile instead of going around, and he was in midstride, his right foot elevated in the air above the gator's back, when the fake performed a most remarkable feat.

The alligator opened its eyes.

Chapter Six

"So how's it goin' to be, bro?" Bear asked.

Blade glanced at the muscular black. They, along with the other Federation delegates, were standing in the hallway outside the conference room. The five faction leaders were in conference behind the closed door. A pair of Free State soldiers, both armed with M-16's, stood at attention outside the room. "I'm going to request M-16's for each of us," he said. "At least four of us will be in the conference room with our leaders at all times. We'll work in shifts."

"They might prefer to conduct their meeting in privacy," Brother Timothy mentioned.

"Tough. We're going to protect them with or without their cooperation," Blade stated. "I don't see where they'd object. At the Home all meetings of the Elders are open to everyone in the Family."

"This isn't the Home," Wolfe's flunky commented.

"The same principle applies," Blade rejoined. "When leaders start holding secret meetings, they breed distrust and a sense of inferiority in those they serve."

"Tell that to Wolfe," the Mole boldly ventured.

"Where's that machine gun of yours?" Bear questioned Blade.

"Back in Minnesota," Blade replied, thinking of his favorite firearm, a Commando Arms Carbine. He'd also used a similar weapon, an Auto-Ordnance Model 27 A-1, for a while. Both resembled the antique Thompson submachine gun. After experimenting with both, he'd eventually decided to incorporate the Commando into his personal arsenal, merely because he liked the feel of the gun a bit better.

"You didn't bring it along?" Bear queried in surprise.

Blade shrugged. He didn't mention Plato had argued

against journeying to California armed to the teeth, as it were, as a show of trust in Governor Melnick and the good people of the Free State of California. Hickok had hotly debated the issue, but Blade had readily assented. Arriving in California packing enough hardware to waste half the state would have been counterproductive to their mission. Besides, in all his years as a Warrior, he had yet to encounter a foe his Bowies couldn't dispatch.

"Who's this?" Bear asked.

Blade looked to the right.

Captain Vinnie Di Nofrio was approaching the conference room, whistling happily.

"It's okay," Blade said. "I know him."

"Blade!" Di Nofrio greeted him. "It's official!"

"It is?" Blade questioned.

"Yep. I've been appointed your liaison for the summit," Di Nofrio disclosed.

"Perfect," Blade said. "As your first official act, you can get M-16's for each of us. And while you're at it, pick up four spare magazines apiece."

Di Nofrio promptly lost his cheery disposition. "I don't know," he balked.

Blade stepped up to the captain and placed his right hand on the officer's slim shoulder. "Now don't disappoint me, Vinnie. I was under the impression you're a real go-getter. You can get the M-16's for us. Clear it with Governor Melnick if you have to."

Di Nofrio's jaw muscles hardened with resolve. "I can get them," he vowed.

"Did you see the attack in the lobby?" Blade asked.

"No. I was in the elevator," Di Nofrio divulged. "But I heard Plato and you were okay. Where's Hickok?"

"I don't know," Blade said, frowning. "He should be back soon."

Di Nofrio started to turn. "Oh! Before I forget. President Toland has arrived in L.A. earlier than expected. Governor Melnick is escorting him here. They should arrive within an hour or so."

"Thanks for relaying the news," Blade said. "And hurry with those M-16's."

"On my way." Di Nofrio hastened off.

"You sure got him eatin' out of your hand," Bear remarked.

"We have this adage at the Home," Blade mentioned. "It goes something like this: If we want to make friends, we have to be friendly."

"Where's the rest of it?" Bear inquired. He'd been through many a battle with the Warriors, both in the Twin Cities and at the Home, and he knew them well.

"The rest of it?" Blade repeated, puzzled.

"Yeah," Bear said. "Your motto should go like this: If we want to make friends, we have to be friendly, but if you mess with us we'll stomp your face."

Some of the others chuckled.

A lean man with black hair and brown eyes, wearing a white shirt and white pants, was walking toward the conference room. He held a tray of water glasses in his right hand.

Blade moved to the conference door, blocking the newcomer's path.

"I beg your pardon," the man said stiffly.

"Who are you?" Blade demanded.

The man in white glanced at the two troopers, then at the giant. "Emery, sir. I'm with the kitchen staff. I was instructed to bring water to the heads of the Freedom Federation and inquire about your culinary needs."

"It's all right, sir," the soldier to the left of the door commented. "He works here. I've seen him before. Yesterday, in fact."

Blade relaxed. "Very well. Go ahead." He stepped aside, to the left, toward the other delegates, and as he did his eyes detected a slight bulge under the kitchen worker's white shirt above the right hip.

Emery was reaching for the doorknob.

"Hold it," Blade said.

Emery paused, looking up at the giant.

"What's that under your shirt?" Blade asked, not really expecting trouble.

Emery's reaction, coming after the confirmation by the soldier, was totally unforeseen. He swept the tray of glasses straight up into the Warrior's eyes, and as the giant instinctively took a stride backwards and raised his right arm to shield his face, Emery went into action. His right hand, the fingers rigid, the callused edge slanted upward, whipped up and around, catching the soldier to the right of the conference door in the throat, crushing the trooper's windpipe, and even as the blow landed Emery was sweeping his right knee in a tight turn to the left, ramming it into the groin of the guard on the left. Before the guard could double over in abject misery, gurgling and sputtering, Emery was in motion, leaping into the air with his right leg snapping out and connecting with Bear's chin, sending the huge black stumbling into his companions.

Hamlin, the small Cavalryman with the Winchester slung over his back, attempted to bring the rifle into play.

Emery landed in a crouch, never hesitating for a moment as he drove his left leg up and around, delivering a high round kick to the Cavalryman's right cheek and knocking him to the floor.

Blade closed in as the man called Emery was trying to grab at somethng under his shirt. The Warrior adopted the Kokutsu-tachi, the back stance.

Emery's right hand emerged from under the shirt gripping a pistol, a Taurus Model PT 92.

Blade automatically performed the Migi-mawashi-geri, a right roundhouse kick, slamming his right foot against Emery's right hand.

Emery lost his grip on the pistol and the Taurus went skidding across the floor. Undaunted, he aimed a Yoko-geri, a side kick, at the Warrior's crotch.

Blade whirled, narrowly evading the foot blow, driving his left elbow down and around in a vicious circle. His elbow caught his opponent above the left eye, staggering him, and before Emery could recover Blade pounded his elbow into the man's face two more times.

Emery staggered backwards, his arms flailing.

Blade didn't let up for an instant. He lashed his right boot in a jamming heel kick, smashing Emery's left kneecap with a loud popping sound.

Emery's left leg buckled and he started to fall.

Blade delivered a haymaker with his right fist to the tip of Emery's chin. The alleged kitchen worker's teeth crunched together, his head jerked back, and he was lifted from his feet and sailed for a yard before crashing onto the floor.

Blade straightened, his hands dropping to his Bowies, scanning the lobby for any more threats. Dozens of soldiers and stunned bureaucrats were staring at him. Otherwise, all appeared normal.

Bear and Hamlin were recovered and glaring at the fallen assassin.

The conference door opened and Plato was framed in the doorway. "What is all the commotion out . . ." he began, then stopped, shocked. "Not again!"

"Again," Blade confirmed.

Bear, rubbing his chin, stood over the unconscious Emery. "What do you want done with this sucker?" he asked.

"We'll interrogate him," Blade said. He knelt next to the soldier slashed in the throat and felt for a pulse. "This one is dead," he announced.

The second guard was doubled over on the floor, clutching his groin. He looked at Blade through pain-filled green eyes. "I don't understand! I know I saw him yesterday in the kitchen!"

"Hang in there," Blade advised. "Help is on the way."

And it was. Troopers and others were converging on the conference room from all points. A stocky officer with a general's insignia on his uniform was the first to reach the prone assassin. "I'm General Gallagher," he declared brusquely.

"General," Blade said. He had seen the general earlier, supervising the cleanup after the lobby attack. Plato had conversed with him briefly, but Blade hadn't had the chance.

General Gallagher moved to the soldier with the crushed throat.

"He's dead," Blade stated.

Gallagher squatted alongside the other guard. "Are you hurt bad, son?" His brown eyes reflected sincere concern.

The second guard groaned, holding his privates. "He . . . kicked me, sir."

"The medics will be here in a moment," Gallagher assured the man. The general peered up at Blade. "Any of your people hurt?"

"No," Blade answered.

Gallagher glanced at the downed assassin. "At least we have one of the sons of bitches alive! I'll get him to talk."

"*We* will question the prisoner," Blade said, disputing him.

General Gallagher rose, his thin lips compressing. "The prisoner is under my authority, and I will handle his interrogation."

"We will," Blade reiterated.

"Now see here!" General Gallagher thundered.

"One moment, gentlemen," Plato intervened, walking from the conference room. "We are allies. We should be working in tandem. Why not interrogate the captive jointly?"

General Gallagher scowled. "I don't need his help, thank you! The Free State Army has functioned acceptably for over a century without the assistance of the almighty Warriors! And we don't want the Family meddling in our affairs!"

Plato and Blade exchanged glances. "Do I detect animosity in your tone?" Plato asked.

Gallagher stepped up to the Family Leader and poked Plato in the chest with his right forefinger. "You're damn right you do, Socrates!"

"My name is Plato," Plato corrected him.

"Whatever you say, Socrates," Gallagher stated sarcastically.

"Why do you dislike the Family?" Plato inquired.

"I'll tell you," General Gallagher replied, jabbing Plato again. "It's not just your Family I don't like. I don't like any of the Freedom Federation clowns! Governor Melnick and his advisors may think signing a treaty with your Federation is essential to California's future, but I don't!"

"Why not?" Plato queried politely.

"We don't need your Federation," General Gallagher declared. "California has managed quite well without you. What can you offer us that we don't already have? Nothing!"

"We offer you our hand in friendship," Plato said. "We will be your allies. We can establish trade routes and mutually benefit from our association in other respects."

General Gallagher laughed. "Trade? What can your Family possibly offer us? It seems to me we're coming out on the short end of the stick."

"Having allies could be crucial should the Soviets, the Technics, or the Androxians decide to attack California," Plato remarked.

General Gallagher snorted derisively. "Let them try! We can defeat any of them!"

"Aren't you being somewhat overconfident?" Plato asked.

"I'm being realistic," General Gallagher snapped. "Our military power is the equal of anyone else's! We're as strong as the Commies or the Technics and the rest, and we're a hell of a lot stronger than the Family." Gallagher snickered. "I've heard all that bull about how great your Warriors are, but I don't buy the lies."

"Our Warriors are quite skilled," Plato commented.

"Your Warriors aren't shit!" Gallagher retorted, poking Plato one more time.

One time too many.

Gallagher was opening his mouth to lambaste the Family Leader some more, when an iron hand clamped on his throat, and a vise grabbed him by the scruff of his neck. He was bodily lifted from the floor and shoved against the wall, scraping his nose and forehead. His neck and throat were released, and he angrily turned to confront his assailant.

Blade loomed above the general, his fists clenched at his sides, his face a livid scarlet. His right arm snaked up, his right forefinger jabbing Gallagher and slamming the officer against the wall. "If you ever lay a finger on Plato again," Blade warned, his voice an ominous growl, "I'll break it off and shove it up your ass!"

General Gallagher couldn't seem to think of what to say. He sputtered, his mouth working like that of a fish out of water, plainly enraged.

"Governor Melnick should be here soon," Blade said. "If you have a complaint, we'll take it up with him."

"I handle my problems myself!" Gallagher stated belligerently.

Blade pointed at the injured soldier. "Why don't you tend to your man, and then get the hell out of my sight!"

Gallagher glared balefully at the Warrior. For a moment, it appeared he would launch himself at Blade. But his attention was fortuitously distracted by the arrival of a pair of medics. "Take care of him!" he barked, indicating the guard, and then stalked off.

Bear moved closer to Blade. "Whew! What got him so bent out of shape?"

"That's what I'd like to know," Blade responded.

"His attitude is most peculiar," Plato agreed. "Perhaps he is an isolationist."

"What's that?" Bear asked.

"Someone who believes a country or state is better off left to its own devices," Plato explained. "They're of the opinion that peace can only be achieved if they do not enter into alliances or make commitments with other nations." He paused. "There were a considerable number of isolationists in the U.S. before the war."

"Could be," Bear said doubtfully. "But if you ask me, that turkey hates our guts."

"I think you're right," Blade said to Bear. "We'll need to keep our eyes on him."

"I will discuss Gallagher's behavior with Governor Melnick when he arrives," Plato mentioned.

Bear gazed across the lobby. "Hey, Blade! Here comes your buddy!"

Blade glanced up, hoping to see Hickok approaching. Instead, Captain Di Nofrio was heading toward them laden with four M-16's.

"He got the guns," Bear remarked eagerly.

Di Nofrio halted, looking at the assassin and the two troopers in amazement. "What happened here?"

"We had a party-crasher," Blade quipped. "You always miss out on all the fun."

Di Nofrio was studying the hit man. "I know him! He works in the kitchen! I saw him serving coffee to General Gallagher when we arrived."

"You don't say?" Blade crossed to the captain and took one of the M-16's. "Thanks for getting these."

"I have two men bringing the rest here in a few minutes," Di Nofrio said.

"Did anyone give you a hard time?" Blade inquired.

"No." Di Nofrio grinned. "I had a call patched through to the Governor's limousine. Only took a minute. The Governor said you're to have whatever you want."

"I'll have to put in a good word to Melnick about you," Blade commented.

"You will? Really?"

"Really," Blade said. He lowered his voice. "What can you tell me about General Gallagher?"

"Why do you ask?" Di Nofrio rejoined.

"I need to know," Blade said. "I take it he doesn't like us."

Di Nofrio nodded. "I heard he argued with the Governor about the treaty we're going to sign. He's dead set against it."

"Why?"

Di Nofrio shrugged. "I don't know. Gallagher has always given the governor a hard time. He's real hard-line military, you know? Sometimes I think General Gallagher would like to be running the state himself. Don't underestimate him, Blade. Gallagher is popular with the troops. General Owens always sided with the governor, which annoyed Gallagher no end. And Owens was just as popular as Gallagher."

"But General Owens is dead," Blade observed. "Who else can keep a rein on Gallagher?"

Di Nofrio pondered for a moment. "No one."

Blade looked at the assassin, reflecting. How far was the general willing to go to insure the treaty wasn't signed? Would Gallagher hire a hit squad to eliminate the Federation delegates? Was the man genuinely concerned about his state, or was the general over the edge, a fanatic?

Someone was nudging his left elbow.

Blade turned, finding Plato at his side.

"Boone," Plato said, pointing toward the rear of the hotel.

The Cavalryman was hurrying toward the conference room, winding through the crowd in the lobby.

Blade moved out to meet him. "Where's Hickok?" he demanded.

"Sorry," Boone said, his mouth curling downward. "I lost him."

"You what?"

"He took off after the man we were chasing," Boone detailed, "and I lost them both. Those gardens back there are a real maze."

"Damn!" Blade muttered. "And I can't leave the summit!"

"I'll keep looking," Boone offered. "Just be sure to let Kilrane know where I am."

"Will do," Blade said. "And thanks."

Boone jogged away.

Blade turned, frowning, telling himself there was nothing to worry about. No one was faster than Hickok. No one was more deadly. So why was he apprehensive? Because Hickok was one of his very best friends? Or because the gunman had this uncanny knack for blundering into dangerous situations? Trouble seemed to be attracted to the Family's preeminent gunfighter like metal to a magnet, and the more bizarre the peril, the more outlandish the jeopardy, the more likely the gunman was to be involved.

Blade sighed. The best he could do was pray Hickok wasn't performing up to par.

Now he was *really* worried!

Chapter Seven

Hickok froze, his right leg suspended above the alligator, his hands inches from his Pythons.

The blamed critter was real!

Hickok was in a quandary. If he planted a couple of slugs in the gator, he'd alert the assassin to his proximity. But he had to make *some* move, and soon! The confounded reptile wasn't going to lie still forever. He realized the alligator had been sunning itself on the bank. Where the dickens could the beast have come from? he wondered. Had its ancestors escaped from a zoo?

The alligator abruptly opened its gaping maw.

Hickok tensed, prepared to draw, but the gator didn't budge. Why in the world was the thing just lying there with its mouth open? Was it trying to catch flies? No. There weren't any flies in January. Was the reptile sunning its teeth?

The alligator grunted.

Hickok couldn't afford to wait any longer. If the alligator wasn't aware of his presence, the thing would be soon. And if the gator knew he was standing here, then either it wasn't hungry or didn't care two hoots.

The gator emitted a loud burp.

Hickok made his move, dropping onto his knees on top of the alligator and sweeping his fists downward, boxing the reptile's eyes, hoping the blows would temporarily obscure its vision. He dived to the right, hitting the turf and rolling, coming erect with the Colts clearing leather and cocked.

The alligator was sliding backwards into the lake, its head disappearing below the water.

Hickok grinned and holstered the Pythons. "Piece of cake," he mumbled.

The water suddenly stirred and rippled, and the

alligator's protruding eyes appeared above the surface.

Hickok braced for an attack, wondering how fast gators could run.

The alligator studied the human for a minute, then sank from sight with a flip of its tail.

"Adios," Hickok said, and resumed his hunt. The lake angled to the northeast, and he began to speculate on whether the lake wasn't really a river.

Buildings loomed ahead.

The structures were in disrepair, consistent with the century of neglect they'd suffered. Windows were cracked or missing, the paint was peeling, and on one of them the roof was crumbling. The verdant forest had reclaimed the land surrounding the buildings, and trees were growing right next to the walls.

Hickok darted from tree to tree, probing for evidence of habitation. The edifices were dark and gloomy. The Warrior circled to the north, 30 feet from the structures. If someone was in there, then they had . . .

Bingo!

Hickok ducked down as he spied a faint light glimmering in the bowels of one of the buildings.

Was it the assassin?

The gunman dashed toward the side of the structure, using the trees and bushes for cover as he zigzagged ever nearer. He reached the wall and pressed his back flush with the wood, listening. All was quiet inside.

So far, so good.

Hickok spotted a door at the top of a ramshackle porch, and he tiptoed up the sagging steps, halting when one of them creaked, then continuing to the door when the creak went unchallenged. Whoever these cow chips were, their security wasn't worth beans!

Someone was talking.

Hickok stopped, cocking his head. The words were muffled, incomprehensible. The door was ajar, revealing a glimpse of a dusty, murky interior. Hickok edged through the doorway, easing the door aside only as much as necessary to permit his passage.

The voice increased in volume, but the individual words were still indistinguishable.

Hickok found himself in a room filled with grime-covered prewar furniture and artifacts. He sidled toward an open door on the opposite side. Bright light was emanating from whatever lay beyond. The gunman warily crossed the room until he was standing behind the open door. He pressed his right eye to the crack between the door and the jamb.

The light was coming from four lanterns hanging from nails which had been hammered into the walls, illuminating a spacious chamber, its windows boarded over, containing tables and chairs.

Hickok's eyes narrowed. He counted nine occupants as well.

There were six men and three women in the room, each one attired in a black robe secured by a thin red sash. Four of the men and the trio of women were seated in metal folding chairs, facing a tall figure. Interposed between them was a man in a soldier's uniform, holding his bloody left arm against his side.

Hickok couldn't see the faces of the men and women in the chairs because their backs were to him. Likewise with the assassin in the trooper's uniform. But the tall figure's features were cast in stark relief by the glow of the lanterns.

The tall one was standing on a crate or wooden box, as if he felt the need to accentuate his already lofty six-and-a-half-foot frame. His hair was auburn, neatly combed and hanging to his broad shoulders. Pale blue eyes were gazing coldly at the one in the uniform. His facial lines exhibited a decidedly sinister aspect. "Explain your failure to us again, Neborak," he demanded in a low, commanding tone.

Hickok saw the assassin in the uniform fidget and glance nervously at those seated to his rear.

"I asked you a question," the tall man reiterated.

"I didn't fail, Kraken!" Neborak blurted. "I know I got one or two of them!"

Kraken raised his right hand and thoughtfully stroked his tapered chin. "Which ones?"

"I'm not sure," Neborak replied.

Kraken's blue orbs bored into Neborak. "You're not sure? How can this be, brother? You just told us you *know* you got one or two of them. Yet you're uncertain of which ones."

"I mean I saw a couple of them fall," Neborak stated hastily. "But I'm not sure which two they were."

Kraken surveyed the men and women in the chairs. "Did you hear Neborak, brothers and sisters? Do his words trouble you as much as they do me?"

"I couldn't stay to verify the kills!" Neborak cried. "I was hit!"

"Ahhhh, yes. Your wound." Kraken gazed at Neborak's left arm. "The elbow, I believe?"

"Yes."

"And who shot you? A Free State soldier?" Kraken inquired.

"One of the Warriors," Neborak answered. "I think it was the one called Hickok."

"You encountered Hickok and you're still alive?" Kraken rejoined. "Most remarkable. Hickok is a formidable adversary."

Hickok nodded. Now he knew who the brains of this outfit was.

"It was Hickok, I tell you," Neborak insisted.

The man named Kraken sighed. "All this prevarication is most distressing."

"All this what?" Neborak asked.

Kraken placed his hands on his hips, the baggy sleeves of his robe draping over his knuckles. "Why don't you reassure us, brother? Go over it again. The Gild will be your judge."

Neborak looked at his seated peers, licking his lips.

"Proceed," Kraken ordered.

"I followed my instructions exactly," Neborak said. "I took one of the uniforms Emery stole for us and met him at the northeast corner of the hotel grounds where they have the garbage cans. I scaled the wall when the guard on the roof was looking the other way, and Emery led me to the rear of the hotel. I stashed my Darter in the garden, in case I needed it for my getaway. Emery took me to a locked closet in a hallway, then unlocked it so I could hide there. There was a fully loaded M-16 in the closet."

Kraken smiled. "Emery is a consumate professional. If

only all the Gild members could be so dedicated to their craft! Go on."

"I waited until Emery came back and told me that Plato and two Warriors had arrived," Neborak said, continuing his narration. "I went to the lobby and shot at Plato and the other leaders. I know two of them went down. Then before I knew it, soldiers were pouring out of the woodwork after me. I barely got out with my life."

"I thought you said Hickok was after you?" Kraken queried.

"He was," Neborak quickly answered. "So were the soldiers."

"This gets better and better!" Kraken said sarcastically. "Now you managed to escape with half the Free State Army and one of the Warriors after you!"

Neborak didn't appear to notice the sarcasm. "I felt it was my duty to return and report."

"Your duty?" Kraken repeated, then said the words again, his voice booming. "*Your duty?* I seriously doubt you know the definition of the word! *Foster* performed his duty, when he blew himself up rather than be taken at the airport. *Emery* is performing his duty by going undercover, by allowing me to plant him on the kitchen staff as our inside man at the hotel. But *you!* You spineless worm! You wouldn't know what duty was if it jumped up and bit you on the ass!"

"Kraken—" Neborak began.

"Silence!" Kraken roared.

Neborak backed up a step.

"I will tell you what you really did!" Kraken bellowed. "I will tell you what really happened! Emery snuck you inside the hotel, as he was supposed to do. And he obtained an M-16 for you, so you could mingle with the other soldiers without drawing attention to yourself. But when it came time for you to terminate the Freedom Federation leaders, you suddenly sprouted a yellow streak down your spine! Instead of mingling and getting as close to the leaders as possible, as ordered, you opened up too soon, and from too far away! Am I right?"

"No," Neborak responded, his voice wavering.

"Don't lie to me!" Kraken admonished. "If you had

gotten as close to the Federation Leaders as you should have been, you would know which ones were dead! And you wouldn't have only shot one or two of them! If you'd been as close to them as you are to me, and if you'd used the M-16 on full automatic, all of the leaders would be dead!"

Neborak retreated another step.

"And after making your ineffectual attempt, you fled!" Kraken stated. "Instead of seeing your mission through to its end or perishing in the effort, you decided your life was worth more than your duty! You've placed a higher premium on yourself than on your membership in the Gild."

Neborak didn't respond.

Kraken's attitude abruptly altered. His shoulders slumped and he sadly shook his head. "I am very disappointed in you, brother. Very disappointed. I expected much better from you. You knew the rules before you entered the Guild. No one forced you to join. No one was twisting your arm. Foster nominated you for membership because he believed you were proficient at our trade. I'm glad he didn't live long enough to discover the error he made."

"Please, Kraken," Neborak said. "Give me a break! I never could have pulled it off anyway! There were too many soldiers there! And the Warriors! At least I tried!"

Kraken straightened. "Any endeavor is a waste if success is not achieved," he philosophized.

"I'll do better next time," Neborak promised. "You wait and see! I'll nail those bastards next time!"

Kraken frowned. "There will be no next time, brother."

"What . . . what do you mean?" Neborak asked tremulously.

"You know what I mean," Kraken stated. He surveyed those seated before him. "Brothers and sisters of the Gild! You have heard the testimony. What is your verdict?"

In turn, each of the men and women extended their right arm, fist clenched, thumb pointing downward.

"The verdict has been rendered," Kraken announced.

"No!" Neborak cried, glancing anxiously about the room as if seeking an avenue of escape from his fate.

"This isn't fair! I should get another chance!"

Kraken looked at one of the seated men. "Nightshade."

Hickok saw the man rise. This assassin was of average height and build, but he wasn't entirely human in appearance. Somewhere along the line his ancestors had been subjected to massive doses of radiation or been exposed to some of the physiology-warping chemicals polluting the environment. His oily hair was coal black, his skin a dark gray. Slanted yellow eyes and a hooked nose dominated his facial features. Prominent cheekbones accented his unnaturally reddish lips. Nightshade was a mutant.

Neborak stared at the hybrid in undisguised fear. "Nightshade! No! Don't!"

The one named Nightshade stood still for a moment, his arms at his sides. Then his right arm swept up, his hand bent vertical.

There was a streak of silver, and a six-inch needlelike shaft pierced Neborak's forehead, snapping his head back. Neborak stiffened, his eyelids fluttering, and then pitched forward.

"Thank you, brother Nightshade," Kraken said. "Now would you be so kind as to dispose of the coward? Feed the corpse to our saurian friend."

Nightshade walked to the body, stooped, and effortlessly lifted Neborak, draping his former comrade over his right shoulder.

Hickok watched Nightshade exit the chamber through a door in the north wall. His eyes narrowed as he spied a row of weapons leaning against the wall near the doorway. The mystery weapons! They were similar to a conventional rifle, with a stock and a barrel, but they were outfitted with an odd, oblong metal cylinder attached to the underside of the barrel in front of the trigger mechanism. A slender tube, apparently utilized to house whatever ammunition the weapon fired, ran from the cylinder to just shy of the tip of the barrel.

"Brothers and sisters of the Gild!" Kraken declared. "Our employer would not be pleased with our performance to date! And frankly, neither am I! We have made three attempts to fulfill our contract, and each one has failed." He paused. "Even discounting Brother Neborak's dismal inefficiency, we are not earning our commission. This is deplorable! The Gild has never failed to execute an assignment, and we will not fail this time!"

"Do you have a plan, Kraken?" asked one of the men in a high voice.

"Of course, Brother Leftwich," Kraken answered confidently. "I will explain my plan in a moment. But first, I need a volunteer to go to the hotel for me. Who will it be?"

Leftwich, a skinny man with a sallow complexion, stood. "I'll go. What needs to be done?"

"You must contact Emery and instruct him to await further orders. I am concerned he might needlessly expose himself to risk, and we can't afford to lose him," Kraken said.

"Emery wouldn't do anything stupid," Leftwich commented.

"Ordinarily, no," Kraken stated. "But he might seek to take advantage of Neborak's blunder. I directed Emery to refrain from becoming actively involved because his inside information is invaluable. But I know Emery, I know his devotion to our Gild. If he thinks there is a chance to achieve our primary goal, he will take advantage of the opportunity. Emery might attempt to terminate the targets himself while our foes are off balance. I want you to take one of the stolen uniforms and go to the hotel. Advise Emery to lay low."

"You can count on me," Leftwich said. He promptly departed through the door in the north wall.

"I have a question, guv," spoke up one of the men in a marked accent. He had curly brown hair.

"What is it, Charley?" Kraken inquired.

"I may be overteppin' my bounds, mate," Charley said, "But I can't help but wonder why the Gild messes with all this piddlin' work when *we* could be callin' the shots? You know what I mean?"

"Our English representative has asked a valid question," Kraken noted.

English representative? Hickok was startled by the revelation. Except for the Russians, he hadn't heard of anyone venturing overseas, or coming from overseas, since the Big Blast. Had England survived the war? And what about the rest of Europe?

"You would like to call the shots, would you, Charley?" Kraken asked the British assassin.

"Of course, guv. Who wouldn't?" Charley responded.

Kraken grinned. "I like initiative in my people. Stick with me and your wildest dreams will come true. We will be calling the shots, as you put it, quite soon. I realize that, on an international scale, the leaders of the Freedom Federation are small potatoes. Very small potatoes indeed. But they are a means to an end. I can't confide all of the details at this time, but rest assured we will see the Gild's power grow to new heights as a consequence of the completion of this contract."

The members of the Gild exchanged puzzled glances.

Kraken noticed. "I can say this," he added to appease their curiosity. "We are receiving more than gold in exchange for the elimination of the Federation leaders. In addition to our standard fee, we will acquire certain information, information which will enable the Gild to become a major player globally. We will become the ultimate power brokers."

Hickok was striving to comprehend the significance of everything he'd overheard. The Gild was obviously an international assocation of professional assassins, and they evidently sold their lethal services to anyone able to meet their price. Less obvious was the reason someone wanted the Freedom Federation leaders murdered. The gunman debated whether to burst into the room, guns blazing, and get as many of the Gild members as he could, or whether to go warn Blade. Even if he managed to gun down these, what if there were others nearby?

Kraken raised his right fist overhead. "To the Gild!"

The Gild members stood and imitated his gesture. "To the Gild!" they echoed.

Hickok backed away from the meeting room. Blade and Plato needed to be informed about the Gild, and he was the only one who could tell them. He carefully inched toward the front door, and he was halfway there when his extraordinary sixth sense, developed over the course of years of fighting experience, flared, alerting him he wasn't alone, that someone else was very, very close. He whirled toward the front door, his hands dropping to his Colts.

One of the Gild members was framed in the doorway, cradling a mystery weapon in his hands. The barrel was fixed unwaveringly on the gunfighter.

With a shock, Hickok realized his path was being blocked by the one known as Nightshade!

Chapter Eight

"One more time," Blade said. "Where are you from?"

"Get screwed!" the assassin retorted angrily.

"This is gettin' us nowhere," Bear commented, hefting his M-16.

They were interrogating the prisoner in a small room on the second floor. The man in the kitchen worker's clothes was tied to a chair positioned in the middle of the floor.

Blade, slowly pacing in front of the chair, glanced at the assassin. "You could make this easy on yourself by cooperating."

"Go play with yourself!" was the response.

"Is your name really Emery?" Blade queried.

"Wouldn't you like to know!" Emery retorted.

Bear, standing to the left of the chair, frowned. "Let me work this sucker over, Blade. He'll talk."

"I'll never talk!" Emery stated defiantly.

Blade stopped and faced the assassin. The cross-examination was getting them nowhere and he had important business elsewhere, namely guarding Plato. He didn't like being away from the Family Leader, not when another attempt could be made on his kindly mentor's life at any moment. And his anxiety over Plato was compounded by his apprehension about Hickok. The gunman had been gone way too long, leaving Blade to conclude Hickok was up to his neck in hot water once again.

Hot water!

Blade motioned for Bear to move away from the chair, and Emery watched them nervously as Blade whispered in the black's left ear.

Bear nodded. "You got it, bro. I'll be right back." He opened the door and departed.

"I'm not going to talk!" Emery insisted. "And nothing you do will make me!"

Blade folded his arms across his chest. "We'll see, tough guy."

Emery attempted to spit at the Warrior, but missed.

"Anyone ever tell you that you have lousy manners?" Blade quipped.

"Joke while you can, prick!" Emery taunted. "You won't be laughing when all of your leaders are dead!"

"I owe allegiance to only one leader," Blade mentioned. "And no harm will befall him while I'm alive." He ran his right hand along the strap of the M-16 slung over his right shoulder.

"You can't stop us, Warrior! No one can!" Emery snapped.

"Thank you," Blade said.

"For what?" Emery rejoined.

"For confirming there are more than one of you left," Blade stated.

"If you only knew!" Emery remarked, sneering.

The sound of a commotion broke out in the hallway outside of the room. Loud noises were raised in argument.

Blade walked to the doorway.

The Cavalryman Hamlin and General Gallagher were involved in a shoving and shouting match. The stocky officer was nose-to-nose with the bantam frontiersman, and neither was giving an inch.

"What's going on here?" Blade demanded.

Hamlin wagged his Winchester at the general. "He wanted in. I told him you said no one was to go inside, but the mutton-head wouldn't listen."

General Gallagher glared at Hamlin. "I'll be damned if a scrawny runt like you is going to tell *me* what to do!"

"You did the right thing," Blade said to Hamlin. He looked at the general. "What are you doing here?"

Gallagher's mouth curled downward. "I came to apologize," he said bleakly.

"You? Apologize?" Blade studied the officer. "Why?"

General Gallagher stared into the Warrior's probing eyes. "Because Governor Melnick just reamed my ass over what happened earlier. He ordered me to apologize. So I'm apologizing."

Blade suppressed a grin. He had to admire the general's honesty. Governor Melnick, accompanied by President Toland and two of Toland's assistants, had arrived a short while ago. Melnick and Toland had immediately repaired to the conference room and joined the other heads of state. Undoubtedly Plato had informed Melnick about the incident with the general, and Melnick had called Gallagher on the carpet.

"I'm not apologizing for what I believe in," General Gallagher said. "I still don't believe in this treaty."

"I'm not asking you to compromise your beliefs," Blade assured the officer. "All I want is for you to give the treaty the benefit of the doubt until it proves itself. The Free State government isn't committed to any specific course of action by signing the treaty, other than agreeing to aid any other member of the Federation should one of us be attacked. What harm can it do to wait and see how the treaty works out before you condemn it? If, six months or a year from now, you feel the treaty has been detrimental to California in any respect, then plead your case before Governor Melnick. Wouldn't he be more inclined to hear you out if you possessed hard evidence supporting your dislike of the treaty?"

General Gallagher appeared surprised by Blade's reasoning. He slowly nodded. "You are a very persuasive man, for a Warrior."

"Thanks. I think." Blade began to reenter the room.

"Wait," General Gallagher said.

"What is it?" Blade asked.

"I'd like to join you, if you don't mind," Gallagher stated.

"Is this an official request from Governor Melnick?" Blade inquired.

"No," General Gallagher admitted. "The governor has no objections to you questioning the prisoner. This is my request. As potential allies, doesn't it make sense to work together on this?"

Blade nodded. "It does. But I'm surprised you'd want

to work with a Warrior. After all, according to you we're not worth shit.''

"Touché," General Gallagher said.

"You really want to work together?"

"I do," General Gallagher confirmed.

"Then let's get at it," Blade declared and entered the room.

General Gallagher grinned at Hamlin and followed Blade.

"Well look at this!" Emery baited them. "They've brought in reinforcements. Where'd you get those bushy eyebrows, general? You look like you're part ape!"

General Gallagher marched up to Emery's chair. "We want answers, and we want them now! Why did you try to assassinate the Federation leaders? We know you were hired to work in the kitchen a week ago. Were you planted here because of the summit?"

Emery snorted. "You don't get nothing out of me, asshole!"

General Gallagher glanced at Blade. "What are we going to do?"

"Wait," Blade replied.

"For what?"

Blade looked at the doorway. "This."

Bear returned, a large pot of steaming water held in his left hand. "Here we go," he said to Blade. "They had this already on the stove, gettin' set for supper."

Blade grasped the pot handle.

Emery was anxiously gazing at the steaming water, his mouth working back and forth, his teeth gnashing together. "What's that for?"

"Guess," Blade said.

"Scalding water won't make me talk," Emery declared, but his tone lacked conviction.

Blade moved over to the chair. He dangled the pot under Emery's chin. "It won't?"

"No!" Emery responded angrily.

"We'll see," Blade commented, leaning down until his eyes were level with Emery's. "Here's the way it is. I need certain information from you, and you will supply the answers one way or the other."

"Don't hold your breath!" Emery scoffed.

"I've questioned a number of prisoners in my time," Blade informed the assassin. "Experience is a great teacher. For instance, my experience tells me you're one tough son of a bitch. Am I right?"

Emery smiled, his chest expanding. "You've got that right!"

"And tough guys like you never, ever talk," Blade went on. "I could tear your fingernails out and you wouldn't cooperate."

"You're not so dumb after all!" Emery jeered.

"I could break your arms and your legs and you wouldn't talk," Blade stated.

"A waste of your time," Emery pompously agreed.

"But I wonder what would happen if I poured scalding water all over your balls," Blade said innocently.

Emery blanched. "What?"

"I wonder how tough you wouldd be if I poured this pot of scalding water on your crotch," Blade repeated.

Emery looked down and gulped. "You wouldn't!"

Blade smiled maliciously. "There's one way to find out."

"You're bluffing!" Emery persisted.

Blade squatted, dangling the pot between his legs. "Unfortunately for you, I'm not bluffing. You see, Emery, I learned an important lesson a long time ago. Most men, no matter how much inner strength they may possess, can not tolerate the thought of having their penis injured." He paused. "How about you, Emery? You're quite skilled at your trade, I'll grant you that. But how devoted are you to your superiors? Devoted enough to suffer the agony of having your pecker blistered by scorching water? Devoted enough to have your balls boiled? Devoted enough to risk possibly never experiencing sex again?"

Emery glared at the Warrior, grinding his teeth.

"I'm going to ask you a question," Blade stated. "If you don't answer, I'm going to pour some of this water on your lap. Ready?"

"Fuck you!" Emery screamed.

"Suit yourself." Blade rose, holding the pot above the

assassin's groin. "Who's behind the assassination attempts?"

"I don't know," Emery responded.

Blade started to tilt the pot of steaming water.

"Honest I don't!" Emery yelled, panic-stricken. "We're never given the identity of our employer in case we're caught!"

Blade hesitated, the pot at an angle, the water near the edge. "You keep using the plural, which means you belong to an organization and you work under someone else. What's the name of the organization? And who is your boss?"

Emery was trying to grind his teeth down to the gums. He stopped, his eyes locked on the pot. "If they find out I talked, they'll kill me!"

Blade went to dump the water.

"Wait!" Emery screeched, his eyes wide. "The Gild! I belong to the Gild!"

"What is this Gild?" Blade queried.

"It's a brotherhood of assassins," Emery revealed, scowling.

"What's the name of your leader?" Blade asked.

Emery shook his head. "I can't! I can't!"

"Suit yourself." Blade tipped the pot.

Emery's neck muscles bulged, his face reddening, as a stream of hissing water splashed onto his lap. The scalding liquid penetrated his kitchen uniform, seeping through the fabric and enveloping his genitals. Emery went crazy, bucking and thrashing against his rope bonds, bouncing the chair, uttering an inarticulate cry.

Blade stopped pouring. He patiently waited until the assassin ceased shaking. "All right. That was just a taste of what will happen if I upend the entire pot. So one more time. What's the name of your leader?"

Emery was sagging in the chair, his face beet red, continuing to gnash his teeth. "Kraken," he said feebly.

"Kraken?"

"That's right," Emery confirmed.

"Where is the Gild based? Here in California? The Civilized Zone? Or in Soviet territory?" Blade asked.

"None of them," Emery replied.

"Then where?" Blade persisted.

"Paris."

Blade did a double take. "Paris, France?"

Emery nodded weakly, his teeth grinding-grinding-grinding.

"You're not French," Blade noted.

"Canadian," Emery said. "I was born in Saskatchewan."

"This Gild is an international organization?" Blade questioned.

Emery nodded.

"How many members are there worldwide?" Blade inquired.

"Thirty-six," Emery replied.

"How many came to California?"

"Twelve," Emery divulged.

Blade's forehead creased as he pondered the news. A brotherhood of assassins! And they had brought one third of their membership to California to slay the Federation leaders, which meant they were determined to see the job through at all costs. But the crucial information was still missing: the identity of the party responsible for hiring the Gild. He heard Emery crunching his teeth together and he gazed down at the assassin, mortified. Why was the man grinding his teeth so much?

Emery unexpectedly straightened, a smile lighting his face. "Finally!" he exclaimed in relief.

"Finally what?" Blade asked.

"Finally I don't need to answer any more of your damn questions!" Emery retorted.

Blade elevated the pot an inch. "You don't?"

"No, bastard," Emery said. "I don't! Go ahead! Pour the water! See if I care!"

Blade was perplexed by the assassin's evident sincerity.

"It should only take a couple of minutes," Emery stated.

"What should?" Blade wanted to know.

Emery grinned. "For me to die."

Blade looked at General Gallagher, who shrugged, indicating he was stumped too.

"You're not going to die," Blade said.

Emery laughed bitterly. "Wrong, asshole! The poison is already in my system. There's nothing you can do."

Blade leaned forward. "Poison? What poison?"

"The poison from the capsule contained in my false tooth," Emery explained.

"You took poison?" Blade inquired in amazement.

"Give the bright boy a prize!" Emery quipped.

"He's bluffing," General Gallagher commented.

"You think so, huh?" Emery said, sneering at the officer. "Shows how much you know."

"That's why you've been grinding your teeth!" Blade deduced. "To break the capsule!"

"To break the false tooth," Emery corrected him. "The damn thing didn't break as easily as they said it would." He chuckled at some private joke. "They extract one of our wisdom teeth and implant a fake containing the capsule. All we have to do is grind our teeth until the fake breaks, and out comes the capsule. One swallow and the job is done." His eyelids began to droop.

Blade placed the pot on the floor and gripped Emery by the shoulders. "What kind of poison is it? There might be an antidote."

Emery tittered. "No antidote."

"How do you know? What kind of poison is it?" Blade pressed him.

"Too late," Emery said, his head nodding.

"Emery!" Blade shook him.

"Let the idiot die," General Gallagher remarked. "It's no great loss."

"We should try to help him," Blade said, straightening.

"Why bother?" General Gallagher countered. "A minute ago you were ready to boil his balls, and now you want to help him? You don't make any sense."

"I was ready to torture him for the intelligence we need," Blade admitted, "but this is different. It's a waste. The Family doesn't believe in meaningless killing."

"But I heard you Family types are real spiritual," General Gallagher observed. "If this son of a bitch has a soul or whatever you want to call it, he'll survive death, won't he? So what's the big deal?"

"A soul only survives if the person possesses faith," Blade stated, watching Emery's mouth twitch.

"Either way, his death will not be any great loss," General Gallagher stated.

Blade gazed at the officer with a stern look of disapproval on his face.

"What's with you?" General Gallagher asked defensively.

Blade crouched, feeling for a pulse. Emery's eyes were closed, his chest immobile.

"Is the sucker dead?" Bear queried.

"He's dead," Blade verified.

"Good riddance," General Gallagher muttered.

"We needed him," Blade stated irritably.

"No we didn't," General Gallagher disputed him. "What's with you? You're the one who's supposed to have killed dozens, maybe hundreds, according to all the rumors floating around. So why are you getting all misty-eyed over one lousy hit man?"

Blade stared at Gallagher. "I'm not getting misty-eyed. When I said we needed him, I meant it. I wanted to discover the location of their local base of operations before they strike again." He paused, sighing. "And as far as the number of foes I've dispatched to the next life is concerned, I haven't counted them. But I do know this. Every time I've killed an enemy, it's been out of necessity, not out of revenge or for the sheer thrill of killing. Every enemy I've faced has been a threat to my Family or myself."

"The noble Warrior, eh?" General Gallagher said, and chuckled.

Blade suppressed his rising temper. "I've been honest with you. Now why don't you be honest with me?"

"What do you want to know?" Gallagher asked.

"How the hell someone as tactless as you ever got to be a general in the first place?" Blade remarked.

Gallagher wheeled and stormed from the room.

Bear laughed and moved closer to Blade. "You sure laid it on that jive-ass honky!"

"I shouldn't antagonize him," Blade commented.

"Don't sweat it, man," Bear said. "The turkey goes around askin' for it. What I want to know is what we're goin' to do next?"

"There's nothing we can do," Blade stated, "except wait for their side to make the next move."

Chapter Nine

Hickok's reaction was as instantaneous as it was unexpected. The assassin had him covered, his Colts in his holsters. No one in their right mind, looking down the barrel of a rifle, would try to buck the odds. By all rights, the gunman should have raised his hands over his head and meekly surrendered. Instead, Hickok relied on his lightning speed to pull his fat out of the fire. The gunfighter threw himself to the right, his right Colt streaking up and out.

Only Nightshade's inhuman reflexes saved him from the Warrior's incredible speed and accuracy. He darted to the left of the door as Hickok's Python boomed, the slug plowing into the jamb a hairsbreadth from his head.

Hickok was caught between the proverbial rock and a hard place. Nightshade would be waiting for him outside if he tried to get away through the front door. And to his rear was a chamber filled with deadly assassins. His agile mind weighed the probabilities, and in the space of two seconds his mind was made up.

The Warrior whirled and dashed into the meeting room.

All of the Gild members were on their feet, staring in confusion at the door in the west wall.

Hickok expected the majority of the assassins to have weapons concealed under their robes. He knew he couldn't nail all off them without being seriously injured or worse. And since his top priority was still to warn Blade and Plato, he had to stay alive if he ever hoped to see them again. Accordingly, as he entered the west door, he was already angling toward the door in the north wall.

The Gild members were highly trained. They overcame their initial bewilderment and went into action. Several ran toward the mystery rifles leaning against the north wall, while others made a grab for arms hidden in their black robes.

Hickok opened up, three shots in astonishingly rapid succession, and the trio of assassins, two women and a man bolting toward the mystery weapons, were downed on the run, each one struck in the head, each one dying in a spray of blood and brains.

"Get him!" Kraken thundered.

Two of the Gild assassins began blasting with pistols.

Hickok was a stride from the north door when the first rounds thudded into the wall, and he ducked and hurtled through the doorway as the Gild members fired in earnest. He was in a narrow hallway leading to an exit door, and he wasn't alone.

The assassin known as Leftwich, the hit man with the sallow complexion, was halfway between the Warrior and the exit. He was alongside a dust-covered clothing rack, in the act of changing from his black robe into one of the four Free State Army uniforms suspended on hangers from the rack. Leftwich was gaping at the gunman in unbelieving stupefaction.

Hickok was about to gun down the skinny hit man when a pistol roared to his rear and a bullet missed his left ear by a fraction. The gunfighter spun, his left Colt belching lead.

A female assassin poised in the north doorway was hit in the left eye, the impact propelling her backward out of sight.

Hickok faced the exit just in time.

Leftwich, a 14-inch survival knife in his right hand, was almost upon the gunman, mere feet away.

Hickok side stepped to the right as the knife sliced toward his face, evading the blow, slanting the Python barrels upward, intending to perforate the assassin's noggin. But the hit man tripped.

Leftwich had been only partially dressed when a solitary shot had sounded from the direction of the west entrance. He'd already removed his black robe and slid into a pair of fatigue pants and combat boots when he'd heard the shot. He'd frozen, his fingers gripping the laces to his right boot, about to tie them, listening. When, just moments later, three shots had thundered in the meeting room, he'd straightened, forgetting all about his untied laces. And now, as he charged the gunman, his oversight saved his life. He tripped on the flapping bootlaces, stumbling forward, past the man in the buckskins, his momentum catapulting him toward the meeting room door in a wild cartwheel of limbs and tangled clothing.

Hickok kept going, sprinting to the exit door and shoving it open.

A weed-choked expanse of ten yards separated the building he was in from several more towering structures. Off to the left was the forest, and to the right, to the east, was dense brush, stands of trees, and a glimpse of another body of water.

Hickok bore to the right, heading for a stand of trees about 40 feet from the door. If he went to the left, he knew he risked exposing himself to the assassin named Nightshade—if the mutant was still near the front porch. By going straight he would have entered one of the other buildings, and he didn't want to be confined with a passel of murderers on his tail. Bearing to the right seemed to be the wisest course. He covered 20 feet with no signs of pursuit, and he was congratulating himself on his brilliant escape from the jaws of death, when there was a buzzing noise close to his right ear and the ground in front of him abruptly exploded, peppering his buckskins with dirt.

Uh-oh!

Hickok ran even faster, glancing over his left shoulder. The silent shot had obviously come from one of the mystery rifles, and since the trajectory went from his ear to the turf, the sniper had to be positioned somewhere far above the ground. He looked up and found his foe, yet another of the Gild assassins on the roof of the building to his left. He realized the guard must have been posted there all along, but had somehow missed spotting his approach earlier. The dense foliage in the forest must have screened him from view from the roof.

The assassin was trying to get a bead on the racing figure.

Hickok weaved to the right, and another section of sod erupted in the space he'd occupied a millisecond before.

The assassin swiveled, trying to compensate for his target's deliberately evasive pattern.

Hickok jogged to the left, then the right again, never

running for more than two steps in a straight line. He was ten feet from the trees when the sniper tried a third time, hitting the ground a few inches to the Warrior's left.

Someone to the rear was yelling.

Hickok reached the stand of trees, diving for cover behind the wide trunk of an oak tree. He flattened on the musty earth, turning to see if they were after him.

They were.

All of them were gathered outside the exit door, checking their weapons. Kraken was barking orders and gesturing angrily. Nightshade stood by his side. Charley, the Englishman, was listening attentively. Leftwich was hurriedly donning a fatigue shirt.

Was that all that were left? Hickok quickly calculated the numbers. There had been nine in the room initially. Neborak had been killed by Nightshade. And he had personally accounted for four of them. So counting the cow chips on the roof, there were five Gild members remaining. Five he knew of, anyway, but there could be more.

Kraken waved his right arm and all four assassins jogged after the Warrior.

Hickok crawled backwards until he was obscured by a thick bush. He rose and ran deeper into the trees, seeking a likely hiding place. How good could the assassins track? he wondered. The soil underfoot was soft and would readily leave prints. He needed a stretch of rocky terrain to throw his enemies off the scent.

More shouting to his rear.

What a bunch of dummies! Hickok chuckled. They weren't making any effort to conceal their pursuit. For professional assassins, these yo-yos were pathetic.

The stand of trees came to an end. Beyond was a section of brush, then more trees, then more water, either another lake or river or the continuation of the one he'd been following after entering the amusement park.

Hickok looked over his right shoulder to insure they weren't gaining on him, then ran toward the line of trees ahead. He hoped he wouldn't stumble on another alligator —or something worse.

The Gild members were making quite a racket, yelling

back and forth.

Hickok paused when he reached the line of trees near the water, glancing back. Why were Kraken and company being so careless? Something wasn't right here. He moved through the trees until he found the lake.

Dominating the landscape to the northeast were a pair of miniature mountains. The highest of the pair was brownish in color, and there seemed to be a half-dozen caves dotting its side. The smaller mountain was a gray spire with a waterfall cascading from its peak to its base. Both mountains were on the far side of the lake. In the middle of the water, and not all that far from shore, was a large island. Docked next to the island's southern bank was a giant antiquated boat.

Hickok eyed the island speculatively. If he could swim to it before the assassins reached the lake shore, they'd never be able to find him. He glanced to the left, and there was a wooden dock projecting into the lake at least a third of the distance to the island.

Perfect!

Hickok sprinted to the edge of the dock. The wood was old and sections were rotted, but the dock appeared to be sturdy enough to support his weight. He tentatively placed his right food on the nearest board to test its strength.

"Any sign of him yet?" bellowed a voice perhaps 30 yards from the lake.

Hickok threw caution to the wind and hastened to the end of the creaking, sagging dock, carefully avoiding ragged holes in the planks, keeping his eyes on the trees behind him. A few small, ramshackle structures bordered the dock, none of which betrayed any hint of recent habitation. He stepped to the very rim and stared at the blue water below. Countless hours of frolicking in the moat at the Home as a child qualified him as a passable swimmer. He could easily reach the island, which was not more than 20 yards from the dock. But he didn't like the notion of getting his cherished Pythons wet. The water wouldn't damage the revolvers, and he would clean them thoroughly at the earliest opportunity, but the idea bothered him and he hesitated.

"Over this way!" someone shouted.

There wasn't any time to taste! Hickok slid his Colts into their holsters, clamped his hands on the grips to insure he didn't lose them, and dropped into the lake feet first. He held his body rigid as the cool water closed about him, keeping his eyes open, and he waited until his descent had ceased before kicking his way back to the surface.

The lake was quiet and peaceful.

Hickok released his Pythons and started swimming toward the island in even, powerful strokes.

"He's heading for the lake!" yelled someone in the trees near the shore.

The assassins were almost to the lake! Hickok swam faster, feeling a clammy sensation as his drenched buckskins clung to him, slightly impeding his progress.

There was a run-down building on the southwest tip of the island. Between the building and the shore, fringing the bank in a verdant cloak, was a ring of dense vegetation.

Hickok marveled at California's prolific plant life. Even in January, which was one of the coldest months of the year back in Minnesota, much of the flora was green and healthy. If he could just reach that bank before the assassins appeared! He looked over his right shoulder as he swam, elated to discover the Gild members hadn't caught up with him yet.

Move!

The Warrior churned the water, his legs and arms pumping, as he rapidly closed the gap to the island. He thought he glimpsed a shadowy form skulking near the building, but when he forced his full attention no one was there.

Must be a case of nerves.

Hickok's moccasins struck bottom when he was eight feet from the bank. He plunged ahead, checking to insure his Pythons were in their holsters, and paddled behind the protective shelter of a clump of overhanging bushes.

Voices rose from the direction of the dock.

Hickok twisted in the water, peering through a crack in the vegetation.

Kraken and the others were standing on the dock.

Hickok waited to see if they were going to come after him. They were gazing at the island, but they weren't acting as if they'd seen him. In fact, they were smiling and joking together. Now what was that all about? he wondered.

A twig snapped behind him.

Chapter Ten

"The jackass fell for it!" Leftwich said, laughing.

"What a bloody twit!" Charley concurred with a snicker.

Kraken gazed at the pair disdainfully. "We were lucky," he declared somberly.

"Why so grim, guv?" Charley asked. "Your plan worked, didn't it?"

"Yeah," Leftwich added. "I've got to hand it to you! When you said we could force him to swim to the island, I figured you were nuts."

Kraken stared at Leftwich until the latter averted his eyes. "I do not make precipitous judgments," he stated testily. "The Warrior had three options. Stand and fight. Try to circle around us. Or keep going until he found a place to hide. By staying on his trail, but not pressing him too closely, and by making enough noise to rouse the dead, we provoked him into doing exactly what I wanted."

"But how did you know he wouldn't stand and fight or try to sneak around us?" Leftwich queried.

"Elementary," Kraken answered condescendingly. "If he'd wanted to stand and fight, he would have done so when he took us by surprise at the meeting, when he had the advantage. And he wouldn't risk trying to return to the hotel until he's certain we're no longer after him." He paused, deliberating. "I suspect he wants to warn the Federation delegates about us."

"And you're positive this bloke is a Warrior?" Charley questioned.

"I recognized him from the file our employer supplied," Kraken said. "He's one of the top Warriors, the one who shot Neborak. He probably followed that imbecile here!"

"You mean Hickok?" Leftwich asked in amazement.

"None other," Kraken confirmed. "And you would

have recognized him too, if you'd done your homework."

"It all happened so fast," Leftwich remarked.

"A lame excuse, if ever I've heard one," Kraken commented.

"Why didn't we just snuff this Hickok ourselves?" Charley inquired. "Why give him to them?"

"I can't afford to lose anyone else," Kraken said. "There are only six of us left to complete the mission." Kraken frowned. "I must have a talk with Farino, and for his sake I hope he has an adequate explanation for his failure to observe Hickok's approach."

"Have a heart, mate," Charley said. "Farino can't be watchin' in every direction at once. He must have been keepin' his eyes on the island, like you ordered. After all, we don't want another run-in with those chaps, do we?"

Kraken studied the island. "No," he agreed. "We must keep them confined to the island until we're done here."

"Should we use the radio and call for assistance?" Leftwich queried.

"No," Kraken replied. "We only use the radio in a dire emergency. I doubt the Free State security forces possess sophisticated monitoring equipment, but we won't take the chance."

"Should I go relieve Farino?" Charley asked.

"Let him stay on the roof for another hour," Kraken said.

The fourth Gild member on the dock, the mutant Nightshade, the silent one, stepped up to Kraken and tapped the Gild leader on the right elbow.

"What is it, brother?" Kraken inquired.

Nightshade pointed at the island, then worked his hands in a series of swift gestures.

"What did he say?" Leftwich probed.

"Nightshade wants to know if we should leave someone near the dock," Kraken said, translating the sign language. "In case the Warrior swims back."

"That's a good idea," Charley said. "Should we?"

"I don't have the manpower to spare," Kraken stated. "But after you relieve Farino on the roof, make damn certain you watch the island closely." Kraken noticed Charley was staring at Nightshade with a peculiar expression. "Is something wrong, Charley?"

"No, guv," Charley responded. "I was just wonderin' what it was like, you know?"

Nightshade's yellow orbs narrowed.

"Nightshade doesn't like to be reminded of his misfortune," Kraken mentioned.

Charley grinned at the mutant. "No offense meant, mate. I was thinkin' about how terrible it would be to have my tongue cut out."

"Nightshade lost his tongue because he was careless," Kraken stated callously. "He barely escaped from the Dragons with his life."

"The Dragons!" Leftwich exclaimed. "They cut out his tongue?"

Kraken nodded. "Nightshade botched an assignment. He was sent to terminate the head of the Dragons, but he was caught."

"Who are these Dragons?"

Leftwich grimaced. "The freakiest bunch of bloodthirsty mutants you'd ever want to meet! I hate them!" He involuntarily shuddered.

Nightshade's right hand unexpectedly flicked out and closed on the front of Leftwich's fatigue shirt. He hardly seemed to strain as he hoisted his fellow assassin into the air.

"Hey! Let go of me!" Leftwich cried, dropping his Darter. "I didn't mean you!"

Kraken placed his right hand on Nightshade's left shoulder. "Release him, brother. He was not referring to you. Leftwich hates the Dragons, not mutants in general."

Nightshade unceremoniously dumped Leftwich on the dock.

Leftwich sprawled onto his buttocks, glaring up at the mutant. "You had no call to do that, dammit!"

"Nightshade is understandably touchy on the subject of mutants," Kraken commented.

"I don't give a shit!" Leftwich snapped bitterly, rising. "We're brothers in the Gild, aren't we? He shouldn't have done it!"

Nightshade's hands performed more sign language.

"He apologizes for his temper," Kraken told Leftwich.

"That's better!" Leftwich said indignantly.

"Now don't you have an errand to run?" Kraken queried.

"An errand?" Leftwich repeated, puzzled.

"Emery," Kraken reminded him.

"Oh!" Leftwich retrieved his Darter. "On my way. I'll tell him to lay low until he hears from you." He ran off.

"So what's our next move?" Charley asked Kraken.

"Governor Melnick is hosting a formal affair tomorrow evening for the Freedom Federation delegates," Kraken said. "He's expected to announce the Free State of California has decided to join the Federation. All of the leaders will be in one place at one time. We'll hit them then."

"It won't be easy," Charley observed. "Security will be exceptionally tight. Why not hit them before tomorrow night? Don't they have some meetings scheduled before then?"

"They do," Kraken disclosed. "But the conference meetings are being held in a smaller room where they're easier to protect. By waiting until tomorrow night, we kill two birds with one stone. First, the formal dinner is being held in a large chamber, increasing our odds of success."

"And secondly?" Charley questioned.

Kraken smiled. "If we don't make any hits until tomorrow night, they might relax their guard a bit. They'll become complacent, wondering why there haven't been any more attempts. Our job will be that much easier."

"How is it, guv, you know so much about their itinerary?" Charley idly inquired.

"I have my source," Kraken said.

"Our employer?" Charley asked.

Kraken nodded. "Our employer has an undercover agent at the summit."

"It sounds to me like you have every angle covered," Charley said, complimenting the chief assassin.

"I always do," Kraken said. He looked at the island. "Let's head on back. We won't need to concern ourselves over the Warrior after tonight."

"Why not?" Charley queried.

Kraken smiled. "Because by tomorrow morning the famous Hickok will be dead."

Chapter Eleven

Hickok turned, his hands dropping to his Colts, scanning the wall of vegetation shrouding the bank.

Nothing.

The gunfighter faced the lake, watching the Gild members. He saw Leftwich leave, and shortly thereafter the others departed. His scheme had worked! Now all he had to do was wait a spell, then swim to the other side and make his way to the hotel to warn Blade. It would be a piece of cake! He decided to find a warmer spot to wait and clambered onto the bank. The brush was dense, and he had to force a path through a thicket and cross a grassy knoll before he discovered an ideal place to rest, a small clearing in a stand of trees. He sat with his soaked back against one of the tree trunks and surveyed his surroundings.

The dilapidated building was in partial view through the trees, about 30 yards to the north.

Hickok sighed, thinking of his beloved wife Sherry and their son Ringo, both expectantly awaiting his return to the Home. He missed them intensely, and he was beginning to understand the reason Blade disliked extended trips away from the compound and the Family. Gallivanting all over the countryside was all right for a single guy, but a married gent needed to consider the impact on those dearest to him.

A bird suddenly whistled to the east.

Only it wasn't a bird.

Hickok leaped to his feet, his blue eyes scrutinizing the landscape. He knew a fake bird whistle when he heard one, and that imitation had been downright pitiful! The gunman listened for the whistle to be repeated or answered from elsewhere in the woods, but all was quiet. He frowned, annoyed by a nagging feeling of being watched. Was it possible the island was inhabited? Had he really seen someone near the building as he was swimming the lake?

There was one way to find out.

The Warrior moved toward the structure, alert for an ambush, his hands near his Pythons.

There was the soft padding of feet from the forest to the northwest.

Hickok halted, debating his next move. He could return to the lake and swim for the dock, but the Gild assassins might still be in the area. He could stay put, but the notion of being a sitting duck was distinctly unappealing. Or he could mosey on over to the building and have a look-see.

Another "bird" whistled to the northwest.

Hickok thoughtfully stroked his moustache. Whoever these hombres were, they knew he was there. They must have observed him crossing the water. He didn't want trouble, but if push came to shove he was prepared to show them the business end of a .357 Magnum.

A bush rustled off to the right.

Hickok hooked his thumbs in his belt and ambled in the direction of the building, his saturated moccasins squishing with every step. No one appeared and he reached the end of the trees unmolested. The structure was ten yards away, a veritable mess; the front door was gone, all of the windows were busted out, and the walls were on the verge of collapsing. He glanced to the right, discovering the large boat he'd seen before, and the sight of the vessel brought a photograph to mind, a picture he'd found in one of the books in the Family library. The photo had been of a steamboat.

More bird whistles broke out in the woods.

Hickok walked toward the steamboat along a well-defined path. The boat was 20 yards or so from the building, adjacent to a tumbledown wooden dock. From the sound of the birdbrains in the forest, he gathered there was a whole flock of the featherless varmints. And if they were out to get him, the boat would be the best spot to make a stand. They would have to cross the dock to reach him, giving him a clear shot.

The steamboat was listing, leaning to one side, inclining toward the dock, as if there might be a hole under the waterline on the island side of the vessel. A gap of four feet separated the boat from the dock.

Hickok reached the dock and stopped. Many of the planks were missing or cracked. He risked falling through the rotted wood if he tried to reach the steamboat, but there was no other choice.

A stooped-over figure dashed between two trees off to the right.

They were getting set to make their move! Hickok moved onto the disintegrating dock, his nerves tingling, advancing slowly. He wondered if he'd made the right decision, if he should chuck the notion and make his stand on the bank. But he was denied the opportunity.

"Get him!" a deep male voice bellowed, and eight forms charged from cover, five men and three women brandishing various weapons.

Hickok spun, his Colts sweeping up and out, cocking the hammers as he cleared leather, and just as he was about to squeeze the triggers, before he could drop a single foe, he was defeated by a weather-beaten, crumbling board. The plank underfoot gave way with a rending crash, and the Warrior plummeted toward the lapping waters below. He thrust his arms horizontal to his falling body, catching himself by his elbows, painfully jarring his arms and shoulders, his Pythons held fast in his straining hands. His lower torso and legs dangled below the dock.

"Don't move, you son of a bitch!" someone commanded.

Hickok looked up to find the barrel of a Ruger rifle a finger's width from his nose. The man holding the rifle was a big man with wide shoulders, a barrel of a chest, a tangled mass of black hair, and dark eyes. His clothing consisted of torn, faded jeans and a crudely constructed deer-hide shirt. Sandals adorned his filthy feet. Hickok mustered his friendliest smile. "Howdy, neighbor!"

The big man blinked several times, his dark eyes narrowing suspiciously. "I ain't your neighbor, bastard!"

Hickok perceived he was as good as dead if he didn't do some real fancy talking, and quickly. "I have this pard with the handle of Joshua. He lives at my Home, and he's the most spiritual person I know. Josh says all of us are neighbors because we all share the same planet. So I reckon we are neighbors, if you get my drift."

The big man leaned down to peer into the Warrior's face.

Hickok nearly gagged when the man's putrid breath assailed his nostrils.

"You're out of your gourd, mister," the man declared.

Hickok grinned, struggling to keep from falling further into the hole. He doubted the cavity was broad enough to permit his shoulders to slip through, but he didn't want to become wedged in more tightly than he already was. "I'd be right grateful if you'd see fit to get me out of this hole."

The big man nodded. "We'll get you out, mister. We don't want to lose you now." He wagged the rifle barrel. "But first you drop them pretty handguns of yours. Nice and easy!"

Hickok hesitated, reluctant to part with his Colts.

"You do it or I'll blow your face off!" the big man threatened.

"I like a man who knows how to motivate folks," Hickok commented wryly. He released the Pythons, laying them on the dock.

The big man straightened. "You might not be as dumb as you look. Tab! Come here!"

A young man joined the big one. The newcomer was a thinner, smaller version of the man with the Ruger. He sported a ragged scar on his right cheek, and was wearing tattered brown trousers with a short black jacket and an outlandish yellow bow tie. A slightly rusted hatchet was in his left hand. "Yeah, Pax?"

"Get this moron's guns," Pax directed.

Tab crouched, warily reaching out and grabbing first one Colt, then the other. He rose, holding them in his right hand. "Wow! These are something else! Can I have one?"

"Maybe," Pax said.

"Those irons are mine," Hickok stated contentiously.

Tab smirked. "Not any more they ain't, mister!"

"You won't be needing them," Pax commented, chuckling. "Jack! Phil! Get this turkey on his feet!"

Two men came forward and brutally hoisted the Warrior from the hole, careful to insure they didn't suffer a similar fate. They rudely shoved him several paces forward onto the bank.

Hickok examined his captors. All eight were on the grungy side, wearing an odd assortment of strange, soiled clothing. The one called Jack was a beetle-browed hulk wearing a faded pink shirt with ruffles down the front, black pants with his knees protruding through irregular holes, and a weird black hat made conspicuous by the yellow skull and crossbones on the front flap. Another man crowned his head with a black cap resembling a set of enormous rodent ears. The three women were dressed equally as bizarrely. One of them was attired in a red and white polka-dot dress and white gloves, while another covered her feet with furry imitation dog paws. "Are you folks tryin' to start a new fashion trend?" he quipped.

Pax rammed the barrel of his Ruger into the Warrior's back. "Shut your face and move your ass!"

Hickok winced, staring at the evident boss. "You touch me with that rifle again and I'm going to cram the barrel down your throat!"

Pax pointed the barrel at the Warrior's head. "Keep flapping your gums and you can die right here!"

"Go kiss a buffalo's butt," Hickok cracked.

Pax angrily motioned with the Ruger. "Move it! Now!"

"Which way?" Hickok asked.

"Follow them," Pax directed.

Four of the motley group were walking to the north along a faint trail.

Hickok fell in behind the four.

"No tricks, mister!" Pax warned, staying behind the Warrior. Tab and two men brought up the rear.

"You mind tellin' me who you people are?" Hickok inquired.

"As if you don't know!" Pax rejoined acidly.

"I don't," Hickok said. "I've never laid eyes on you before."

"Bullshit!" Pax declared bitterly. "You saw all of us a week ago!"

"I've never seen you before," Hickok reiterated. "I wasn't even in California a week ago."

"What's a California?" Pax queried.

Hickok glanced over his right shoulder. "You're joshin' me, right?"

"My name's not Josh," Pax responded.

"You really don't know what California is?" Hickok questioned in disbelief.

Pax shook his head.

"The Free State of California is the name of the state you live in," Hickok explained.

"What's a state?" Pax wanted to know.

Hickok's brow creased in bewilderment. "You mind settin' me straight on a few things?"

Pax scrutinized the man in the buckskins. "Like what?"

"Can you read?" Hickok inquired.

"What's that?" Pax responded, the Ruger barrel fixed on the prisoner's back.

"Do you know what a book is?" Hickok asked.

"Nope," Pax replied.

"Ain't them those things we use to help get the fires started sometimes?" Tab chimed in.

"Those things?" Pax said. "We don't see many of them in the Kingdom anymore."

"The Kingdom?" Hickok repeated quizzically.

"The Kingdom, mister," Pax stated. "Where we live. This place."

"You call this old amusement park the Kingdom?" Hickok remarked. "Why?"

"I don't know nothing about no amusement park," Pax asserted. "This place is our home. It's always been called the Kingdom. That's what my dad called it and his dad before him."

"How long have you folks lived here?" Hickok asked.

"Our families have lived here since doomsday," Pax answered.

"Doomsday? You mean World War Three?"

Pax shrugged. "Call it whatever you want, mister. My dad told me all about it. A long, long time ago, in the land outside of the Kingdom, everybody was trying to kill everybody else. Doomsday, my dad called it. The end of everything. We've been here ever since."

"Your family, your ancestors, hid out in the park during

the war and stayed here after it was over," Hickok reasoned aloud.

"Of course we stayed here in the Kingdom," Pax said. "Where else would we go?"

"There's a whole wide world out there," Hickok stated. "You should see it sometime."

Pax made a snorting sound. "Who are you trying to kid? We know what's out there! Poison air and poison ground. Killers and robbers. And lots of mutants. We wouldn't last a day out there, mister."

"You can call me Hickok," the gunman suggested. "Where'd you ever hear the world is as bad as all that?"

"From my dad," Pax said. "His dad passed it on to him. We know we're safe in the Kingdom and we're never going to leave."

"You've got to leave sometime," Hickok advised. "You'll be surprised to find out that the folks out there aren't half as bad as you make 'em out to be. Not all of 'em, anyway."

"Yeah. Sure. And I suppose you and your friends are a good example, huh?" Pax demanded testily.

"My friends?"

"Don't play innocent, you son of a bitch!" Pax exploded. "We don't know how all of you got in, but a week ago Chester found the bunch of you staying in that building on Orleans Square. We spied on you for two days, watching you come and go. You bastards with your black robes and puff guns!"

Puff guns? Hickok realized the man was referring to the Gild members' favorite weapons, the Darters.

"Chester was all for being friendly," Pax was saying. "He said we shouldn't kill you before we found out what you wanted."

"What happened?"

"You know damn well what happened!" Pax snapped, his face livid. "You shot Chester and three of our brothers and drove us to the island! You would have caught all of us, but you didn't know we had canoes on the north shore."

Hickok contemplated Pax's disclosures. No wonder

these people hated his guts! They believed he was part of the Gild, and the Gild had tried to wipe them out.

"We've been watching you on and off ever since," Pax went on. "No one knows the Kingdom like we do. We can spy on you anytime. You ain't such great shakes!"

"And I saw what you did to those three outsiders," Tab mentioned. "I followed one of your scouting parties."

"You never should have left the Kingdom," Pax said reproachfully.

"I wanted to see what they were up to," Tab explained. "They didn't go very far. I think they were just looking around to see what was out there." He paused, frowning at Hickok. "I never did see no sense in why those three people were killed."

"Don't look at me," Hickok said. "I'm not one of the Gild."

"What's the Gild?" Pax inquired.

"They're the varmints who gunned down your kin," Hickok said.

"And you ain't one of them?" Pax asked skeptically.

"That's what I've been tryin' to tell you," Hickok stressed.

"You expect us to believe you?" Pax retorted resentfully.

"I'm tellin' the truth," Hickok averred.

"Lies won't save you," Pax declared. "We're going to pay you back for what you did to Chester and the others."

"You'd kill an innocent man?" Hickok asked.

"Doesn't matter to us whether you're innocent or not," Pax said.

"Why not?"

Pax grinned, exposing his discolored teeth. "Because we're hungry."

Chapter Twelve

"You shouldn't leave the grounds, sir," the lieutenant warned. "It could be dangerous out there."

Boone gazed at the brick wall, his brown hair waving in a gust of wind, his brown eyes studying the red streak before him. "If Hickok went over, then I'm going over."

The lieutenant in charge of the cleanup detail shook his head. "I can't stop you, but I don't think you're doing the right thing."

Boone stared at the corpse lying at the base of the wall. A pair of soldiers were wrapping their deceased comrade in a body bag.

"We don't really know if the Warrior went over the wall," the lieutenant noted.

"There's nowhere else he could have gone," Boone countered. "I know he's not in the hotel, and I've searched the garden from one end to the other. Hickok isn't on the grounds. He was after the hit man. If the trail of dead soldiers ends here, then the assassin went over the wall at this spot and Hickok followed him."

"If you're determined to see this through," the lieutenant offered, "I can go with you."

"Thanks, but no," Boone said. "I can make a lot faster time by myself. But you can do me a favor."

"Name it."

"Find Blade, the other Warrior," Boone directed.

"The one with all the muscles?" the lieutenant queried.

"That's him. Tell him where I've gone, and ask him to relay the news to Kilrane. He'll understand."

"Will do," the lieutenant promised. He moved next to the wall and cupped his hands at his waist. "Can I give you a boost?"

"Thanks." Boone placed his right moccasin in the officer's hands and nodded.

The lieutenant heaved.

Boone sailed upward, easily gripping the top of the wall and sliding over to the far side. He landed upright, his hands on his 44 Magnums. He had to find Hickok, if only to redeem himself in his own eyes. If he hadn't rushed headlong into the garden in pursuit of the Warrior and the assassin, if he'd only paid more attention to their tracks and less to keeping Hickok in sight, he wouldn't have lost them. His stupidity bothered him, and he knew he wouldn't live it down if the Warrior was killed.

The Cavalryman crouched and examined bootprints and moccasin tracks, both leading off to the northeast. Elated his hunch had been right, Boone rose and jogged across the field. He found an animal trail in the forest beyond and ran along the path until he reached an obstruction, a chain-link fence covered with plant growth.

Now which way? he wondered.

Boone spotted a hole in the vegetation and squatted to peer through it.

A flock of sparrows perched in a tree on the far side of the chain-link fence suddenly broke into flight, chirping wildly.

Boone stood, listening. A lifetime on the Dakota plains had taught him to recognize and react to the subtle signals nature provided. Something had spooked the sparrows, but what? He detected the pounding of feet coming from the other side of the fence, and he quickly moved to the right and ducked around a thick bush.

A moment later a head poked through the hole in the fence. A thin man in a soldier's uniform crawled into view with an unusual rifle slung over his left shoulder.

Boone was on him while the man was still on his hands and knees, pressing the barrel of his right Hombre against the startled crawler's left ear.

The man stiffened and gasped.

"Howdy," Boone greeted him. "Who are you?"

"Leftwich," the man blurted. "Private Leftwich. I was sent out to look for the guy who tried to kill the leaders earlier."

"I don't think so," Boone said.

"Why don't you believe me?" Leftwich asked in annoyance.

"For starters your rifle isn't Free State Army issue," Boone mentioned. "I've never seen a gun like it. What is it?"

Leftwich clamped his thin lips together.

"Suit yourself," Boone said, his right foot lashing forward.

Leftwich was struck in the ribs. He grunted and tumbled onto his right side, wheezing, clutching at his chest.

Boone leaned over the sickly-looking man. "One more time. What kind of rifle is that?"

"A Darter!" Leftwich replied breathlessly.

Boone reached out and tapped the oblong cylinder under the Darter's barrel. "This is what was used on the soldiers in the garden, and somebody tried to kill me with one of these. What's it shoot?"

"Explosive darts," Leftwich revealed, grimacing in pain.

"You don't say," Boone commented. "How?"

Leftwich was rubbing his left side. "Compressed air. The Darters are accurate up to one hundred yards. Semi-automatic or full auto."

"Do they explode on contact?" Boone inquired.

"They detonate on penetration of the target," Leftwich detailed.

Boone straightened. "Slip your Darter to the ground."

Leftwich slowly removed the sling and gingerly deposited the Darter on the grass.

Boone squatted, his right Hombre trained on the assassin, and lifted the Darter in his left hand. "I'll hang onto this for you. Stand up."

Leftwich complied, his eyes pinpoints of hatred.

"Where's Hickok?" Boone asked.

"I don't know any Hickok," Leftwich answered.

"Suit yourself," Boone said. He backed up several strides.

"I don't know any Hickok!" Leftwich reiterated.

"Does your mom know she raised a chronic liar?" Boone commented. He checked the Darter and found a safety located over the trigger. "Is this thing loaded?" he questioned while flicking the safety off.

Leftwich's beady eyes widened. "Be careful with that!"

Boone aimed the Darter at the assassin's head. "I think I'd like a demonstration."

Leftwich glanced from the Darter to the Hombre. "I don't know where Hickok is! Honest! He got away from us!"

"Us?"

"The Gild," Leftwich disclosed.

"You're going to take me to where you last saw Hickok," Boone ordered. "If I suspect you're playing me for a fool, I'll shoot you with your own gun."

Leftwich scowled. "This just isn't my day," he muttered.

Boone holstered his right Magnum, gripping the Darter with both hands. "After you." He indicated the hole in the fencce with a sweep of the barrel. "Stay on your hands and knees when you get to the other side. Don't stand until I tell you to."

Leftwich knelt next to the hole. "Who are you? Another Warrior?"

"No," Boone replied.

"You look like one," Leftwich said.

"Through the hole," Boone stated. He crouched and watched Leftwich obey, then went through himself. "On your feet," he commanded, rising.

"Now what?" Leftwich asked.

"I told you. Take me to where you last saw Hickok," Boone directed.

Leftwich dejectedly started off.

Boone refrained from interrogating the phony soldier, concerned their voices might attract unwanted attention. The assassin could be questioned after Hickok was safe and sound. He followed Leftwich to a lake, then north along the shore. When they reached a large gray beast in a stand of trees, he halted. "What's that?"

"An artificial elephant, you hick," Leftwich responded.

"Wasn't civilization grand?" Boone remarked. "Keep going."

Leftwich headed toward tall structures to the northeast.

As he trod on the heals of the weasel of an assassin, Boone reflected on the chain of circumstances resulting in his presence in the Free State of California. Five years ago, before the Cavalry had made contact with the Family, prior to the Cavalry joining the Freedom Federation, his life had been much simpler. Boone had been raised on a ranch in central South Dakota, and he deeply missed those relatively carefree days spent as a young horseman on the plains. He enjoyed fond memories of his four brothers and three sisters, and he looked forward to seeing them again in June at the annual Boone reunion. They would swap tales about their experiences during the past year, and his brothers and sisters would undoubtedly pester him, as they had done the past five years, to hear about his exploits. They were undeniably proud of the degree of notoriety he had achieved as best friend and chief adviser to Kilrane, the Cavalry leader. Not to mention his fame as a pistoleer.

Boone disliked his fame and the consequences of having an exaggerated reputation. He sighed, thinking of the time four relatives of the previous Cavalry leader had attempted to bushwack Kilrane. Instead, the simpletons had caught Boone in their trap, and he had slain all four in a stand-up gunfight. That unfortunate incident had increased his celebrity tenfold, and Boone had resented every undeserved iota of attention. Killing someone was not his idea of a worthwhile accomplishment, not an act to be extolled to high heaven. He knew Hickok actually relished his renown, and he couldn't comprehend how the Warrior could abide all those overstated stories and fawning idiots a man with a rep inevitably encountered.

Give him the bouncing rhythm of a sturdy stallion, the comfortable feel of a well-worn saddle, and a cool breeze on his face! He longed for the good old days, the days before the Cavalry joined the Federation, when there were less complications. As Kilrane's right hand and personal bodyguard, Boone was entrusted with protecting his friend at all times, including the periodic extended trips to attend Federation Council meetings. Initially, when the Federation had first been formed, Boone had liked the traveling, the meeting of new people, and the making of new friends. But enough was enough! Five years of being at Kilrane's beck and call, five years of living an unsettled existence, five years during which his own ranch had suffered from neglect and his relationships with the fairer sex had fizzled to zero had all taken their toll. He was eager for a prolonged rest, a chance to work on his spread and court one of the local ladies. And he promised himself he would bring the matter up with Kilrane at the first opportunity.

They were about a hundred yards from the buildings.

"That's where I last saw Hickok," Leftwich said, pointing at the second building from the right.

"In there?" Boone questioned skeptically.

"That's right," Leftwich maintained. "He attacked us, then took off. The last I saw him, he was going into the tunnels."

"What are the tunnels?" Boone queried.

"There's a whole network of them under those buildings," Leftwich said. "I don't know who dug them. I only know they're there."

"He must be out of there by now," Boone commented.

"Maybe not," Leftwich said. "Those tunnels are a damn maze. It's real easy to get lost down there."

A maze? Boone thoughtfully gazed at the structures. He'd used the exact same word a short while ago to describe the gardens behind the hotel. Was it possible Leftwich was telling the truth, that Hickok was lost in an underground labyrinth?

"Do you want me to show you the spot where I last saw the Warrior?" Leftwich asked.

"Not so fast," Boone said. "I want to know how many Gild members are around here and where they are right this minute."

"There's two more here," Leftwich lied. He waved his right hand to the east. "They're off that way, over by the old plaza."

There was movement on the top of the second building from the right.

Boone glanced up, hoping to find Hickok, but all he saw were a pair of pigeons flying from the roof.

"Do you want me to take you or not?" Leftwich inquired impatiently.

"Lead on," Boone directed. "But there'd better be some sign Hickok was there. Tracks, anything."

"I think you'll be surprised at what you find," Leftwich declared.

They slowly approached the second building.

Boone held the Darter in his left hand while his right rested on the corresponding Hombre. He didn't trust Leftwich for a minute! He recognized the slim likelihood of Leftwich being honest, but he couldn't afford to discount the murderer's information on the off chance of finding Hickok.

Leftwich angled toward the open door in the middle of the west wall of the second building. "We go in there."

"You go first," Boone ordered. "And no funny stuff!"

"Wouldn't think of it," Leftwich assured him, but as he turned toward the door he grinned maliciously.

Boone warily followed the assassin. If he was walking into a trap, he was going to be certain to use the Darter on Leftwich before they got him. He briefly wished he'd undergone the extensive combat training Hickok, Blade, and the other Warriors had experienced. As was typical of the majority of Cavalrymen, he was a rugged individualist capable of surviving by relying on his wits and his strength, on his prowess at fisticuffs and his exceptional talent with his Hombres, but his actual combat experience had been limited to the war years ago between the Civilized Zone, then ruled by a dictator, and the other factions which later combined to form the Freedom Federation.

Leftwich reached the open door and glanced over his left shoulder. "Stay close," he said. "I wouldn't want to lose you."

"I'll be right behind you," Boone said.

Leftwich walked into the gloomy interior.

Boone took a tentative step forward, and his hesitancy saved his life.

A burly man with curly black hair, dressed in a flowing black robe secured by a red sash, lunged from the shadows to the right of the doorway, in the act of swinging a short curved sword at the Cavalryman's head. But the Gild member had misjudged his swing, excepting his adversary to be a full stride inside the door.

Framed in the doorway, Boone threw himself backwards, the sword arching past his face and deflecting off the Darter barrel. He took two strides and leveled the Darter as his assailant charged after him.

The assassin raised his sword for another stroke.

Boone fired from the hip. There was no retort, no recoil, but the Darter was supremely effective and exceedingly lethal.

The burly assassin twisted to the right as the explosive dart penetrated his pelvic wall above the crotch and detonated, showering his kidney, intestines, and black fabric outward. Screeching, he doubled over, his face inches from the Darter barrel.

Boone squeezed the trigger again.

A spume of crimson, flesh, and gray and white matter burst out of the top of the assassin's cranium and he tottered backwards, flopping onto his back.

There was no sign of Leftwich.

Boone was about to plunge into the building after the devious killer when a pair of steely hands fastened onto his back, one at the waist and the other on the nape of his neck. He was savagely wrenched into the air and shaken like a child's rag doll.

"Get the bastard, Nightshade!" Leftwich cried, emerging from the structure.

Boone was slammed onto the ground, onto his knees, and he attempted to turn, to bring the Darter to bear. But a dark gray hand appeared from his rear and yanked the rifle from his grasp.

"Waste him!" Leftwich shouted in delight.

Boone rose and spun, his hands diving for his Hombres, but as fast as he was his opponent was faster. And what an opponent! Oily black hair, hooked nose, slanted yellow orbs, and gray skin, all trademarks of a genetically altered being, a mutant.

Nightshade grabbed Boone around the waist, pinning the Cavalryman's arms, and hoisted him into the air.

Boone struggled in vain to break free. The mutant was endowed with incredible brute force!

"Kill him!" Leftwich cackled.

"No!" thundered a new voice.

Boone saw a towering man with pale blue eyes and auburn hair come into his line of vision from the left.

"Why not, Kraken?" Leftwich asked the newcomer.

Kraken stared at Leftwich, his jaw muscles twitching. "Because I said so! Do you need a better reason?"

"No," Leftwich responded meekly.

Kraken studied the figure in Nightshade's clutches. "You're a Cavalryman, aren't you?"

Boone didn't answer.

"Nightshade," Kraken said.

The mutant applied pressure on Boone's back, squeezing until Boone thought his spine was on the verge of snapping. Boone's face reddened and he gasped for air.

"Enough," Kraken stated.

Nightshade relaxed his brawny arms.

"Obstinacy will gain you nothing," Kraken said to Boone. "Nightshade will break you like a twig if you don't cooperate." He paused. "Are you a Cavalryman?"

Boone nodded, striving to suppress an acute pain in his chest.

"What's your name?" Kraken asked.

The information was hardly worth dying for. "Boone," the Cavalryman replied.

"Ahh, yes. I've heard of you," Kraken mentioned. "A competent man in your limited way. You're Kilrane's bodyguard, or at least one of them." He gazed at the dead Gild member. "I might have granted you a quick death, but you've killed one of our brothers."

"Let me have him!" Leftwich requested.

Kraken glanced at Leftwich in stern disapproval. "I noticed you managed to get yourself captured."

Leftwich blanched. "He got the drop on me!"

"Obviously," Kraken said.

"It won't happen again," Leftwich asserted.

"I hope not," Kraken stated, "for your sake." He looked at Boone. "Considering the level of incompetence demonstrated by my colleagues on this assignment, perhaps I should change our name from the Gild to the Simpletons."

Boone said nothing.

Kraken sighed. "A keen sense of humor is so seldom

appreciated." He gazed at Leftwich. "Go up on the roof and tell Charley to come down here. We are going to move our temporary base of operations to another part of the park. This place is prone to too many unwelcome guests."

Leftwich ran into the building.

"And now to decide your fate," Kraken said to Boone. "Your killing of Farino necessitates a gruesome demise. The code of the Gild and all that."

"Why do you want to kill the Federation delegates?" Boone ventured to ask.

"I head an organization of professional assassins," Kraken replied. "The answer should be readily apparent."

"Someone must have hired you," Boone noted. "Who?"

Kraken grinned. "That information is classified." He looked at Nightshade. "Do you think our saurian friend might enjoy some dessert?"

The mutant smirked.

"Bring him," Kraken directed, walking to the north.

Nightshade carted the Cavalryman without appearing to exert himself.

"As I was saying," Kraken said over his right shoulder, "your killing of our brother Farino necessitates a fitting death. The Gild firmly believes in the ancient adage of an eye for an eye. Since you used a Darter on Farino and blew him to pieces, so to speak, it is only fitting you suffer a similar fate."

Boone was endeavoring to quell a rising tide of panic. He desperately wanted to pry himself loose from Nightshade's grip, but the mutant's arms were like bands of iron. His fingers were touching the grips on his Hombres, yet the revolvers might as well have been on the moon for all the good they were doing him. What use could they be if he couldn't move his hands to draw them?

"The second day after we arrived in the park we discovered we had a next-door neighbor," Kraken was saying. "You'll be interested in meeting him, I'm sure. Or should I say meeting 'it'?"

"They'll come looking for me," Boone stated.

Kraken chuckled. "Perhaps. But by the time they do, we won't be here and you will be in the belly of Leviathan."

"The belly of what?" Boone queried.

"Why, I'm surprised at you," Kraken said as they rounded the northwest corner of the building and walked toward a marshy track to the northeast. "Haven't you read the Holy Bible?"

"The Bible? I've read parts of it," Boone stated. "What's the Bible have to do with this?"

"Have you ever read Job?" Kraken inquired.

"Years ago," Boone disclosed. "When I was a kid."

"And you don't remember Leviathan?" Kraken said mockingly. "Well, never fear. You're about to have your memory refreshed."

They traversed a field and reached the bank of a large pool of brackish water.

"This swamp encompasses several acres," Kraken divulged. "The water is drainage from the lake over there." He pointed to the east.

Boone glanced in the indicated direction and spotted a lake containing a big island.

"Do you see the island?" Kraken asked.

Boone nodded.

"The one you were seeking, the Warrior Hickok, is on that island," Kraken said.

"How do you know I was looking for Hickok?" Boone questioned.

Kraken stared at the Cavalryman. "Please. Don't insult my intelligence." He surveyed the bank. "I see Leviathan has disposed of poor Neborak. The beast might not be hungry again for some time, but I trust you won't mind the wait?"

Nightshade suddenly snapped his head back, then forward, butting his forehead against the Cavalryman's chin.

Boone felt his teeth mash together as excruciating agony lanced his jaw and face. He was unceremoniously dumped onto his stomach on the hard earth and his arms were jerked behind his back.

"Secure the bonds tightly," Kraken ordered.

Boone felt his wrists being lashed together and he tried to resist, but the mutant held him as easily as a cougar could control the feeble escape attempts of a fawn. His legs were roughly bent at the knee and his ankles were tied.

"That should suffice," Kraken said.

Boone shook his head, clearing his mind. He strained, looking over his right shoulder and discovering a single leather cord had been used to bind both his wrists and his ankles. Six inches of cord separated his hands from his feet. His legs were bent backwards.

Kraken knelt alongside the Cavalryman. "An ingenious technique," he commented. "If you try to straighten your legs, you must dislocate your arms in the process. And should you try to extricate your hands, you will tear the hell out of your knees. Either way, the torture will be exquisite."

Boone glowered at the Gild chief.

Kraken straightened. "This park abounds in wildlife. Some of the animals are quite unique. I imagine the abundant vegetation and the water attracted them." He grinned at Boone. "When we scouted the terrain after our arrival, we discovered a few mutants had taken up residence. This is an ideal habitat because there are very few humans here. As soon as Leviathan is hungry again, you will get to meet one of the mutants." He chuckled. "In parting, allow me to wish you bon appétit." He laughed at some private joke.

Boone watched Kraken and Nightshade walk off toward the buildings. He craned his neck, getting his bearings. His feet were a yard from the pool, his head angled up the slightly sloping bank. He estimated he was 40 yards from the nearest building. The cord securing his wrists was tied so tightly his forearms were tingling. Amazingly, they hadn't taken his Hombres. But the guns were useless unless he could free his hands. He tried to wriggle his wrists from side to side in an effort to loosen the cord, only his wrists wouldn't budge. How long, he wondered, before Leviathan showed up? A sound behind him drew his attention.

There was a commotion in the center of the pool, an underwater disturbance causing concentric ripples to fan outward.

Boone tensed. Was it Leviathan?

As if an answer to his silent query, a huge reptilian back broke the surface of the water.

Chapter Thirteen

"I'd like you to meet my assistants," President Toland said.

The summit delegates were gathered in the hotel lobby for a period of socializing while the leaders enjoyed a much-deserved break. Members of the kitchen staff were circulating around the room, offering snacks and drinks to everyone. Free State soldiers ringed the lobby, each one armed with an M-16. In the southeast corner Blade and Plato had been discussing Hickok's prolonged absence when they were approached by the president of the Civilized Zone and two others.

President Toland was wearing a brown suit tailored in the prewar fashion. He gestured at a woman to his left. "Plato, may I introduce Melissa Parmalee. Her official title is Administrative Assistant to the President. She handles the thousand and one petty details I can't afford to waste my time with, like scheduling my itinerary on trips and arranging my accommodations."

Blade studied the woman. Parmalee was about five feet eight, her figure slim and shapely. Her attire consisted of a smart red dress and jacket. The dress reached to her knees and her ample cleavage was discreetly covered by her jacket. He received the impression she was a very dedicated, very businesslike woman who relied more on her brains than her physical charms. Her hair was a sandy blonde, her eyes brown.

Parmalee offered her right hand to Plato. "I'm pleased to meet you. I've heard many flattering things about you from President Toland."

"The pleasure is mutual," Plato assured her, shaking.

Parmalee faced Blade. "Is this who I think it is?"

President Toland laughed. "This is Blade, the head Warrior. I'm sure you've heard of his exploits."

Parmalee nodded, seemingly impressed. "That I have. The man who can change the course of rivers with his bare hands," she said grinning.

Blade shook her hand, chuckling. "I gave up changing the course of rivers," he quipped. "It was dirty work. I kept getting my clothes all muddy."

President Toland indicated a man standing to his right. "And this is Frank Ebert, my Federation Liaison. He's responsible for insuring all Federation business is treated expeditiously. He was instrumental in finalizing the details for this summit."

Ebert was a short man, about five feet in height, and his features were on the pudgy side. His hair was brown, as were his eyes, and he was wearing a green suit. "I'm happy to meet you both at last," he commented in a low voice. He shook hands with Plato, then Blade.

"Is Hickok still missing?" President Toland asked.

Blade frowned. "Yes. Boone went after him, but neither of them has returned yet."

President Toland gazed about the lobby until his blue eyes alighted on General Gallagher, who was engaged in conversation with Governor Melnick. "I understand you've assumed command of the security detail for the summit," he remarked. "I overheard General Gallagher complaining to the governor."

Blade shrugged. "Couldn't be helped. I hope I didn't cause any problems for you."

Toland smiled. "Not at all. In fact, I was glad to hear it. I only pray there are no more attempts on our lives." He paused, chewing on his lower lip. "Speaking of security, I'd like to go over the setup for the banquet tomorrow night."

"Fine with me," Blade said.

"Will you excuse us for a moment?" President Toland said to the others. Then he led Blade off by the arm.

"You don't need to worry about the banquet," Blade stated. "I've issued M-16's to all of the delegates and we will personally guard the entrances to the banquet room."

"I'm not worried about the banquet," Toland revealed. "I drew you aside to discuss something else."

"What?" Blade asked.

President Toland stopped and checked to make sure no one was in their immediate vicinity. "I want to discuss the spy."

Blade's mind flashed back to the Russian officer captured near the Home. The officer had revealed there was a Communist spy in President Toland's administration.

"Before I go any further, I want to ask you a question," Toland said. "Who do you think is responsible for the assassination attempts on the summit leaders?"

"I don't know," Blade responded. "The Freedom Federation has made several enemies over the past five years. There are the Androxians in Houston, the androids who want to rule the world. And the Technics in Chicago want to see us destroyed. Not to mention the Soviets. Any one of them could be behind the effort to disrupt the summit. Or it could be a new enemy."

"Don't you have any idea which one it may be?" President Toland inquired, his blue eyes conveying his concern.

"If I had to make a guess, I'd say the Russians," Blade speculated. "But any one of them could have hired the Gild."

"Yes, General Gallagher told me all about your interrogation of the one called Emery," Toland said.

Blade thoughtfully stroked his chin. "Hmmm."

"What is it?" President Toland queried.

"I just thought of something."

"What?"

"Emery told me the Gild is based in Paris, France," Blade mentioned.

"So?"

"So whoever hired the Gild must have the means of traveling from the continental U.S. to Europe," Blade deduced. "And we know the Soviets lack the capability. The Russians possess a lot of functional helicopters, but no jets, so far as we know. And the Technics don't have an Air Force or any craft able to make a transatlantic voyage. But the Androxians do. So I could be wrong. The Androxians might have hired the Gild."

"Unless, of course," President Toland observed, "the

Gild has a North American office or headquarters or some means of being contacted here."

"That's another possibility," Blade admitted.

"Which brings us to the spy," Toland stated. "I must make a confession." His mouth curled downward. "I expected the summit to become the target of some form of attack."

"You did? Why didn't you inform us?" Blade demanded.

"Put yourself in my shoes," President Toland said defensively. "The more people I told about the summit, specifically about the summit's location, the greater the likelihood of the information falling into hostile hands. By the same token, the more people I told about expecting an attack increased the probability of our unknown enemies refraining from mounting an attempt if they knew we were anticipating one. Do you follow me so far?"

"I think so," Blade responded.

"My strategy was simple," Toland explained. "I knew the spy would consider the summit information crucial. I believed the spy would pass on the location of the summit to the Russians. And I knew full well the Russians wouldn't hit the summit if they knew we were prepared for them."

"I'm beginning to see what you're driving at," Blade commented.

"So while I told no one about expecting an attack," Toland elaborated, "I did confide in a few close advisors about the summit's location. That way, if an attack was made, I'd know one of the people I confided in must be responsible for relaying the information to the Russians, must be the spy."

"Pretty clever," Blade admitted. "But what if whoever is behind the assassination attempts received the news through another source?"

"That's possible, I suppose," Toland conceded.

"How many on your staff knew the exact location of the summit site?" Blade asked.

"The two envoys I initially sent to California were aware of the selected site," Toland detailed. "But both of them are completely reliable. I've known them since we were children in Wyoming."

"Who else?" Blade probed.

"General Reese, whom you know," Toland said.

"And I can't see Reese being the spy," Blade declared.

"Me neither," President Toland agreed. "Which leaves just two other people I told."

"Which ones?" Blade inquired.

President Toland turned and nodded toward Plato, Parmalee, and Ebert. "Guess."

"Parmalee and Ebert?"

"Exactly," Toland confirmed. He looked at Blade. "One of them is the Russian spy. I'm certain of it."

"And you want me to find out which one," Blade deduced.

"Can you?" President Toland asked.

"I'll give it my best shot," Blade promised. "But the job won't be easy. I'm going to have to be rough with them. I can't use kid gloves. And if they're innocent, they might resent the treatment and blame you."

President Toland stared at the floor. "It can't be helped. We know there's a spy in our midst and we must discover the agent's identity before irreparable harm is done to the Freedom Federation."

"Since I have your permission, I can get started right away," Blade said.

"Is there anything I can do?" Toland queried.

"Yes," Blade stated. "In about fifteen minutes send one of them up to Room 212, the room I interrogated Emery in."

"Which one do you want first?" Toland questioned.

Blade scrutinized the two bureaucrats. "Send up Ebert first."

"He'll be there in fifteen minutes," President Toland assured the Warrior.

Blade glanced at the Civilized Zone's leader. "I hope you're right. If you're not, there are two people who might wind up hating you."

"Don't you think I know that?" Toland responded. "But preserving the Federation must take precedence."

"If it's any consolation," Blade offered, "I agree with your decision."

President Toland stared at his two advisers, then at Blade. "It's not."

"You know the old saying," Blade remarked.

"Which one?" Toland wanted to know.

"It's lonely at the top."

Chapter Fourteen

This was another fine mess he'd gotten himself into!

Hickok was trussed up like a wild animal ready for slaughter. His shoulders ached from the strain of bearing all of his weight. The wind was increasing in intensity, the gusts causing him to spin. He faced north, then east, then south, then back to the north again, and he frowned as he surveyed the preparations for the feast at which he was going to be the main course.

Lousy cannibals!

The gunman had encountered cannibals before, during his two runs to the Twin Cities. And there were stories about other human maneaters, bands of them roving the countryside and pouncing on hapless wayfarers, and isolated colonies where unwary travelers were lured in, slain, and consumed. Despite the prevalance of such tales, Hickok had never gave them much credence.

Until now.

One of the Family Elders had once discoursed on the subject. The Elder had chronicled the history of cannibalism and emphasized several salient points. Cannibalism had been part of the religious and social mores in primitive society, and at one time had been almost universal among the early races. And in periods of supreme stress, during war or drought or any other calamity, to avert starvation some people reverted to the primeval practice of eating their fellows. The aftermath of World War Three had been a case in point. Millions suddenly found themselves without food as the distribution network collapsed. Where formerly they could waltz into the nearest supermarket or restaurant and glut themselves on their favorite foods, they abruptly discovered the realities of life without a fast-food outlet. Relatively few prewar citizens had bothered to stockpile provisions in case of an emergency. Consequently, they were compelled to roam the land seeking whatever sustenance they could find. Even those skilled at hunting and fishing were hard pressed to keep food on the table when the environment was so drastically polluted by the radiation and the chemicals, thereby contributing to a massive kill-off of game.

Hickok stared at his captors. Their ancestors must have sought refuge in the amusement park during the war and stayed, isolating themselves from the world outside, eating anything and everything they could scrounge up. Perhaps there hadn't been many animals in the park right after the war. Perhaps, unable to grow their own food in sufficient quantities to assuage their constant hunger, they had turned to another food source: picking off anyone who ventured into the park. Once started, the practice must have passed from generation to generation and been accepted as normal behavior. Ironically, when one of them had finally opted to break with tradition and make peaceful overtures to others in the park, the dummy had picked the Gild. And not wanting witnesses to their operation, the assassins had killed poor Chester and three others and driven the rest into hiding on the island. So much for brotherhood.

Hickok felt the rope chafing his wrists. His captors had led him north across the island until they had reached an astonishing structure. Hickok had gaped at it in stark wonder. He'd seen the like before, in photographs and paintings in books in the vast Family library. Among the hundreds of thousands of volumes personally selected by the Founder, Kurt Carpenter, were dozens dealing with life in the Old West. A number of them dealt with Western history, detailing the spread of the white man as he drove the Indians from the Plains. And during the course of his reading, Hickok had seen photos and reproductions of the typical forts utilized by the U.S. Army. But never in his wildest dreams had he ever expected to find himself *in* one!

His captors had taken refuge from the Gild in a decaying fort on the north side of the island. The fort was complete with four guard towers, one at each corner, and a spacious cental compound with headquarters, a barracks, and a corral. The fort was in terrible shape, with most of the wood used in its construction blistered or warped. The front gate, located on the south side of the compound, lacked the large left door, which was laying in the dust inside the fort. The cannibals had produced a 20-foot length of stout rope and proceeded to loop the rope over a beam on the ramshackle rampart above the gate. Next they had bound their victim's wrists and raised him into the air, dangling him three feet above the ground in the middle of the gate opening, where they could keep an eye on him while readying their meal.

How the blazes did he get himself into these fixes? Hickok saw the one called Pax walking toward him. There were 14 cannibals in the fort, including 4 women and 4 children. Tab was strutting around the compound with the Pythons stuck in his frayed leather belt.

"What do you want, you polecat?" Hickok demanded as Pax drew near.

Pax had his rifle slung over his right shoulder. He stopped and looked up at the prisoner. "Are you hungry?"

"What?" Hickok thought his ears were deceiving him.

"Do you want something to eat? We have some root soup," Pax offered.

"You eat it," Hickok told him. "You're going to need your strength when I come gunnin' for you."

"You must eat something," Pax declared.

"Why all this fuss over givin' me a meal? What difference does it make?" Hickok asked.

"The women don't like you," Pax stated.

"Well don't take this personal," Hickok retorted, "but your womenfolk aren't exactly the pick of the crop."

"The women say you're too skinny," Pax elaborated.

"So?"

"You're all muscle," Pax said. "And we don't care for stringy meat."

"Then find somebody with a pot belly," Hickok snapped. "And cut me loose."

"The women think we should hold onto you for a while," Pax disclosed. "Fatten you up in the meantime."

"Your women sure are a bunch of sweethearts," Hickok cracked.

"It's up to me to decide," Pax said.

"Don't rush on my account," Hickok recommended.

"I just don't know," Pax stated uncertainly. "We could all use a good feed."

"How can you do it?" Hickok inquired.

"Do what?" Pax responded.

"What do you think, you cow chip! How can you go around eatin' folks?" Hickok asked irritably.

"When you're hungry, you're hungry," Pax answered.

"Yeah, but eatin' other *people*!" Hickok scrunched up his nose. "Yuck!"

"Don't you eat people?" Pax queried in surprise.

"Are you crazy? Of course not!" Hickok retorted.

"You should try it sometime," Pax suggested.

"Don't hold your breath," Hickok said.

"You'd like it," Pax asserted. "Human flesh is quite tasty. It's better than deer meat."

"There's no way I'd eat a fellow human," Hickok declared distastefully.

"Ain't you the noble one?" Pax said sarcastically. "I've got news for you. If you had a choice between starvation or eating someone, you'd eat."

"Bet me."

Pax inspected the Warrior's frame. "Trying to fatten you up would take too much time. I think we'll have you for supper."

"Tonight?" Hickok asked.

"Tonight," Pax confirmed, starting to turn away.

"I hope I give the whole bunch of you diarrhea!" Hickok stated.

Pax gave a little wave of his left hand and smirked. "Be eating you!" he said cheerily, then walked off.

Mangy coyote! Hickok felt a blustering blast of wind strike his back. His body swayed, then turned as the rope twisted. He was facing to the west this time, and he beheld a dark, roiling cloud bank filling the western horizon.

A storm was coming.

Perfect!

Just what he needed!

As if it wasn't bad enough he was going to be eaten by a

group of looney-tunes, now he was about to be rained on in the bargain!

Some days it just didn't pay to roll out of the sack!

Chapter Fifteen

Other eyes were also gazing at the approaching frontal system.

"Look!" Kraken declared, pointing to the west.

The Gild members, their arms laden with Darters, uniforms, and supplies, were tramping to the east, seeking another suitable temporary headquarters.

"It's a storm, guv," Charley commented.

"So what?" Leftwich chimed in.

"So the elements themselves are working in our favor," Kraken said.

"How do you figure?" Leftwich inquired.

"This storm is an unexpected ally," Kraken stated. "We can use it to our advantage."

"What do you have in mind, mate?" Charley asked.

"We're going to change our plans," Kraken replied. "We're going to hit the Federation leaders this evening."

"But I thought you wanted to hit them tomorrow night," Charley observed.

Kraken glanced from Charley to Leftwich. "What is the distinguishing earmark of a professional in our trade?"

"Skill with weapons," Leftwich replied.

"Smarts," Charley opined.

Kraken sighed and shook his head. "Wrong, brothers. The distinguishing earmark of a true assassin is adaptability, being able to adjust according to the constantly shifting circumstances you're confronted with, being able to modify your plans to suit the situation."

"I knew that," Leftwich stated.

Kraken looked at Nightshade, who grinned.

"This storm is a godsend," Kraken informed them. "I estimate the front will arrive here in about two hours, just about the time it gets dark. The storm will enable us to easily penetrate hotel security. Terminating the leaders will be a simple task."

"Are all of us going in at once?" Charley queried.

"Yes," Kraken responded.

"Shouldn't we hold someone in reserve, just in case?" Charley questioned.

"No," Kraken answered. "We've tried sending in one at a time and the strategy hasn't worked. We'll go after them in force. There are enough Army uniforms left to go around."

"What about the motorcycles?" Leftwich asked.

"What about them?" Kraken countered.

"Are we going to leave them stashed in the Plaza?" Leftwich inquired.

"The bikes will remain where they are," Kraken said. "Once the delegates have been terminated, we will return to the amusement park, retrieve the cycles, and head for the coast. The sub is waiting for our signal. We can be on our way home by tomorrow morning."

"What about Emery?" Leftwich questioned. "I never did get to contact him and tell him to lay low."

"We'll find him tonight," Kraken stated.

"I'm looking forward to some action," Charley remarked.

Kraken swept them with a somber stare. "Before we go into action, I must reiterate the essentials of our contract. We have been hired to terminate all of the Freedom Federation leaders. But should the circumstances prevent us from killing all of the leaders, we are to concentrate on hitting the most important ones. You've all read the file. Which three leaders must be terminated at all costs?"

"Toland, the president of the Civilized Zone, is one of them," Leftwich noted.

"And Plato, the head of the Family," Charley said.

Nightshade, holding two Darters tucked under his left arm, moved his hands in sign language.

"Yes," Kraken said. "The third one is Governor Melnick. Our employer does not want the Free State of California to join the Freedom Federation. So remember the description provided in the file. Plato, President

Toland, and Governor Melnick must be killed no matter what. The rest are not as crucial."

"Don't fret, guv," Charley commented. "All their bloody leaders are as good as buried."

Chapter Sixteen

"You wanted to see me?" Frank Ebert inquired, standing in the doorway to Room 212.

"Come in," Blade said. "Have a seat."

Ebert hesitated.

Blade was standing next to a chair in the center of the room. The rest of the furniture, except for a double bed behind the chair, had been removed to Room 213 prior to Emery's interrogation.

Ebert, his pudgy features betraying a hint of nervousness, glanced at the big black nonchalantly leaning against the wall to the right of the door. "Who's this?"

"This is Bear," Blade said, introducing his friend. "He's from the Clan."

"Yo, bro," Bear said, smiling pleasantly.

"Pleased to meet you," Ebert said, looking at the M-16's both men carried slung over their right shoulders and sounding slightly anxious.

"Have a seat," Blade repeated, motioning toward the chair.

Frank Ebert frowned as he entered the room. He crossed to the chair and slowly sat down. "What is this all about?"

Blade nodded at Bear, who closed the door and faced them.

"President Toland said there's something I may be able to help you with," Ebert mentioned.

"There is," Blade acknowledged, stepping in front of the chair and locking his eyes on Ebert's.

"What is it?"

"We need to know your reporting procedure," Blade stated matter-of-factly.

"To President Toland?" Ebert said, puzzled.

"No," Blade replied, leaning forward. "To your Soviet superiors," he said, grinning, never expecting the reaction he provoked. He had not bothered to tie Ebert's hands and feet, partly because he had to assume the bureaucrat was innocent of espionage until proven guilty—and he didn't want to use excessive force right off the bat, and partly because he was overconfident. Blade stood a good two feet taller than Ebert, and his bulging muscles dwarfed the rotund administrator's. He didn't consider Ebert as much of a threat, and his blunder cost him.

Frank Ebert's right shoe swept upward, catching the Warrior in the groin and doubling him over.

Bear straightened, grabbing for his M-16.

Ebert was faster, his right hand streaking under his green jacket and reappearing with a small automatic. "Don't move!" he barked, pressing the pistol against Blade's forehead.

Bear froze in the act of unlimbering his M-16.

"Drop the gun," Ebert commanded, but Bear didn't move.

Blade, his face a deep scarlet, was gasping and covering his crotch with his hands. The agony in his testicles was excruciating.

Ebert stood, keeping the automatic touching Blade's head. "Drop it or I will shoot."

"You don't have no silencer on that peashooter," Bear noted. "You shoot Blade and you'll have all the soldiers in the world in here."

"But Blade will be dead," Ebert rejoined. "And his death will be on your hands. Now drop the damn gun!"

Blade looked at Bear and nodded.

"You're callin' the play," Bear said, and allowed the M-16 to fall to the carpet.

"Now I want yours," Ebert instructed Blade.

The Warrior grimaced as he unslung his M-16 and handed the weapon over.

Ebert took the gun in his left hand and flicked off the safety. He moved to one side and leveled the M-16 at Blade. "Okay. You're going to be my passport out of here."

Blade grit his teeth and rose to his full height. "You'll never make it," he predicted.

"You let me worry about that," Ebert snapped. "We're

going to walk out of the hotel together. I want you to stay three feet in front of me the whole time. One wrong move, if you make a peep, I'll kill you. Understand?"

"I understand," Blade said.

"Drop your Bowies," Ebert directed, then abruptly changed his mind as the Warrior gripped the hilts of the knives. "No! Keep them! Just don't touch them on the way out!"

"You don't want them?" Blade asked in surprise.

"Everyone knows how attached you are to those Bowies," Ebert stated. "If you were to walk through the lobby without them, one of your friends in the Federation might become suspicious. So just keep your mitts away from them and you may live long enough to see your wife and son again."

"You seem to know all about me," Blade observed.

"You don't know the half of it," Ebert responded. He wagged the M-16 in the direction of the door. "Move your ass."

Blade shuffled toward the door, his movements awkward because of the lingering torment in his gonads.

Ebert slid his pistol under his jacket. "Move out of the way," he ordered Bear.

The Clan member moved away from the door, his hands in the air. "I don't want no trouble. Just don't shoot Blade."

"Your loyalty is touching," Ebert commented sarcastically. He cautiously skirted the black and walked to within a few feet of the Warrior.

Blade took hold of the doorknob.

"Wait!" Ebert commanded.

Blade turned.

"We're going to close the door behind us," Ebert said to Bear. "Keep it closed. I'll keep looking back, and if I see the door open I'll kill Blade. Understand?"

Bear nodded.

"I'd shoot you now, but like you said, the soldiers would be here in seconds," Ebert remarked.

"I hope we meet again some day, sucker," Bear said. "And you don't have no guns."

"The feeling is mutual," Ebert retorted. He looked at

Blade. "Remember what I said. Keep your hands away from those knives. Act natural. We'll go downstairs and cross the lobby. I'll release you once we're outside and I'm safe."

Blade was feeling his strength return as the discomfort in his privates subsided. "I'm ready," he said.

"Then let's go," Ebert declared.

Blade exited the room.

Ebert followed, lowering the M-16 to his side and closing the door shut after casting a meaningful warning glance at Bear.

Hamlin, the Cavalryman, was on guard, standing to the right of the doorway. "Everything okay?" he asked Blade.

"Fine," Blade said, walking down the corridor.

Ebert smiled at the frontiersman and strolled after the Warrior. "Head for the elevator," he said when they were out of earshot from the Cavalryman.

Blade nodded, moving down the hall to the elevator located on the north side of the building. Although several soldiers were lounging in the corridor, none were near the elevator doors. He reached out and pushed the down button.

"No tricks once we're in the lobby," Ebert warned.

"I wouldn't think of trying something," Blade lied.

The elevator arrived, the doors swishing open.

"After you," Ebert said.

Blade entered and stepped to the rear.

Ebert, warily watching the Warrior, came inside and stood next to the control panel. He punched the white button marked with an L.

"You surprise me," Blade said as the elevator began to descend.

"Why?"

"I guess I expected you to allow yourself to be tortured to death before you'd admit to being a Russian spy," Blade stated.

Ebert made a snorting noise. "Where'd you ever get a dumbass idea like that?"

"I read this book when I was a kid," Blade divulged. "A spy book from the fiction section of the Family library. I can't recall all of the plot, but it had something to do with this spy called Bond. He was tortured, but he didn't talk."

Ebert snickered. "You Family types will believe anything, won't you? That prewar nonsense doesn't apply to real life. I'm not about to die for the Russians!"

"You're not willing to die for the greater glory of Communism?" Blade quipped.

"Don't make me laugh!" Ebert snapped. "I'm in this for two reasons. One of them is the money."

"The Soviets are paying you to spy?" Blade asked.

"Why do you sound so surprised?" Ebert responded. "The Russians want to destroy your Freedom Federation, and they will go to any lengths to achieve their goal. They need inside information, so they prepped me and sent me into the Civilized Zone to infiltrate President Toland's administration. It was easy as pie! Qualified personnel are hard to come by, and the Russians made damn sure I was qualified, complete with a phony background, before they sent me out."

"Wasn't your background checked?" Blade inquired.

"Are you kidding? Toland's personnel director asked me a few questions, gave me some tests, and that was it! They never suspected a thing."

"What were you before you became their spy?" Blade queried.

"None of your business," Ebert responded.

The elevator reached the lobby.

"Not one false move," Ebert warned, hefting the M-16.

The elevator doors slid open. Blade walked out, heading across the lobby toward the front entrance. Clusters of soldiers, bureaucrats, and others were engaged in conversation here and there, but not one gave him more than a passing glance. The Federation leaders and Governor Melnick were already back in conference.

Ebert stayed to Blade's right, two strides away, the M-16 at his side, his finger on the trigger.

"There's something I don't understand," Blade mentioned, wanting to draw out their discussion. The more he talked, the more he distracted Ebert, the more likely the spy was to slip and give him the opening he needed.

"What?"

"Why didn't the Soviets send in one of their officers to do the spying?" Blade asked.

"How do you know I'm not an officer?" Ebert rejoined.

"You don't impress me as the military type," Blade said.

"I'm not," Ebert conceded. "The decision to send in a spy was made after your buddy, Hickok, escaped from General Malenkov in Washington, D.C. Malenkov wanted to learn all he could about the Federation. The Soviets could have used one of their own officers, but let's face facts. The Russian officers, even those they raise and educate after impregnating American women, are real stuffed shirts. They can follow orders blindly, but they're not known for their imagination and inventiveness. And Malenkov wanted someone devious, someone who was your basic sneaky type, someone familiar with life on both sides and able to mingle undetected. Back in the old days he could have used an expert, someone trained in one of the Russian spy schools. But they don't have those schools here, not yet anyway. So Malenkov decided the best candidate would be a professional smuggler."

"You were a smuggler?" Blade said.

"That's right," Ebert affirmed, his expression saddening. "One of the best. There's a big market for scarce commodities, goods you can hardly find anywhere because of all the shortages. Neither the Russians or the Civilized Zone have much of a manufacturing capability. The people can never get enough of what they want. And that's where I come in. Or came in. I supplied customers on both sides with whatever I could get my hands on. I was doing real well too. I had scores of contacts, I knew all the safest points to cross the borders, and I was accumulating quite a hoard of gold and silver." He sighed. "And then the Russians pulled the plug."

"They caught you?" Blade deduced.

"They caught me," Ebert said. "Not only that, they traced me to my home in the Outlands, the area between the Civilized Zone and the Soviet-occupied territory. They captured me and my whole family. My wife and three kids," he revealed in a melancholy tone.

"What happened then?"

"The Russians offered me a deal," Ebert disclosed. "Malenkov offered to spare the lives of my family if I'd spy for him. He also agreed to pay me more gold than I could make in ten years of smuggling. There was nothing I could do but say yes. What choice did I have?"

"And you expect General Malenkov to honor your deal?" Blade queried skeptically.

Ebert frowned. "Not really. He's a lying bastard! But what else could I do? He has my family!"

They were almost to the front entrance. Blade glanced over his left shoulder at the novice secret agent. "Don't you miss your wife and kids?"

"Of course!" Ebert snapped. He morosely, absently gazed at the floor.

Which was the opening Blade was waiting for. He spun and leaped, executing a flying tackle, his muscular arms encircling Ebert's waist, his momentum carrying both of them to the carpet with the spy on the bottom.

"No!" Ebert cried.

Blade straddled the former smuggler, pinning the man's wrists to the floor with his powerful hands.

"No!" Ebert thrashed and kicked. "Don't! The Russians will kill my family if they find out I've been caught!"

"How do you know they haven't already?" Blade asked. "When was the last time you talked to them?"

Ebert ceased resisting, releasing his grip on the M-16. "Sixteen months ago," he said softly.

Soldiers were running toward the pair, and one of the fleetest was General Gallagher. "Blade! What's going on?"

Blade scooped up his M-16 and stood. "We've caught a spy."

"What?" General Gallagher drew a pistol from a flapped holster on his right hip.

Ebert made no attempt to move. "I'm dead," he stated dejectedly. "And so's my family!"

"Maybe not," Blade said.

Ebert rose to his elbows. "What do you mean?"

"Have you ever killed anyone for the Russians?" Blade queried.

"No," Ebert replied with conviction.

"This man is a Russian spy?" General Gallagher interrupted.

"Stand up," Blade ordered, ignoring the general.

Ebert complied.

"Why have the Russians hired the Gild?" Blade asked.

"The Gild? I never heard of it," Ebert answered.

"You've never heard of an organization of assassins known as the Gild?" Blade elaborated.

"Never," Ebert replied. "If the Soviets hired this Gild, no one ever told me about it."

"How would you like a chance to see your wife and children again?" Blade inquired.

Ebert's forehead creased in confusion. "What are you talking about? You know I want to see them again."

"If you'll cooperate with us," Blade said, "I'll see that you're released from custody. The rest will be up to you. You'll have to find where they're holding your family and free them yourself. You might be able to pull it off if the Soviets don't know you're free, if they think you're still in the Civilized Zone spying for them."

"You'd let me go?" Ebert responded in amazement.

"Now wait just a damned minute!" General Gallagher interjected. "If this man is a spy, you don't have the authority to release him."

Blade stared at the general. "Must we go through this again?"

"But you can't simply let him go!" Gallagher protested.

"I'm not just letting him go," Blade stated impatiently. "I said I would release him if he cooperates with us."

"In what way?" Ebert asked.

"You were a smuggler for years, right?" Blade questioned.

"For seventeen years," Ebert replied.

"So you must know the Soviet territory better than most people," Blade noted. "And you also know all the best spots to cross the Soviet borders undetected. Did you spend time in Washington?"

"Yes. When they were preparing me for this assignment," Ebert responded.

"Then you must be familiar with the Soviet chain of

command," Blade observed. "Not to mention other valuable information."

"I know a little," Ebert stated.

"Then here's the deal," Blade said. "If you'll agree to cooperate, if you'll let General Gallagher and myself interrogate you, if you'll honestly answer every question, then I'll persuade President Toland to release you as close to the Russian territory as possible. What do you say?"

Ebert's face was a curious contrast of commingled hope and doubt. "You'd do this for me? Why?"

"Because I have a family of my own," Blade declared.

Ebert nodded. "All right. You have a deal. I'll help you if you'll help me." He paused, peering into the giant's grey eyes. "And I want you to know I'll never forget this. If there's ever anything I can do for you—anything—just say the word."

"I'll keep it in mind," Blade said.

"One thing," Ebert mentioned quizzically. "How did you know I was a spy? What tipped you off?"

"You did."

"Me?"

Blade grinned. "I had no idea you were the spy until you kicked me in the nuts."

Ebert was flabbergasted. "Well I'll be damned!"

"He kicked you in the nuts?" General Gallagher queried.

"Yep," Blade responded.

Gallagher shook his head. "I'm beginning to wonder about you Warriors."

"Wonder about what?" Blade asked.

"First you get all misty-eyed over Emery taking poison, and now you're all set to let a spy go. And he kicked you in the nuts, yet you don't do a thing to him!" Gallagher shook his head again. "I'm beginning to wonder if all you Warriors are nothing but wimps."

Chapter Seventeen

The storm struck southern California with a vengeance. Hickok, exposed to the elemental fury, was seething inwardly with an intensity equal to the storm's. Ever since he'd arrived in California, there had been one setback after another! First, he'd missed the clown on the terminal roof at the airport. Then he'd nearly been blown to smithereens when the limo was hit. He'd almost been caught by the Gild, and to top everything off he'd gone and gotten captured by a group of illiterate cannibals!

Why did everything always happen to *him*?

The cannibals had taken shelter in the barracks. Driving sheets of rain pelted the ground and smacked against the fort. The gusting wind was whipping the trees surrounding the fort, bending the saplings almost in half.

Hickok swayed and rocked, soaked to the skin, vowing to get even with the varmints responsible for his latest humiliation. He glared at the barracks, wishing one of them, just one, would come outside and walk up to him so he could kick the crack-brained moron in the head!

One did.

Then another.

Hickok squinted, striving to see through the wall of rain. The landscape was plunged into a watery gloom by the combination of the storm and the twilight.

Two of the cannibals were walking his way.

Hickok tensed expectantly. What was up? Were they coming to kill him for the evening meal? He recognized the one called Tab, and he restrained an impulse to yell with delight when he spotted the pearl handles of his Colts sticking from Tab's belt. He shifted his attention to the second cannibal, his eyes blinking in astonishment.

Was that a chicken?

The second cannibal was wearing torn, ragged jeans, a faded blue shirt with large white buttons on the front, and some kind of bizarre headgear. He looked for all the world like a fuzzy white chicken with a yellow bill. Only this bird was carrying an axe in his right hand.

Just when you think you've seen everything!

Tab and the second cannibal halted a yard from the swinging gunman, Tab with a carving knife in his left hand. He smirked at the Warrior. "Guess what time it is?" he shouted above the wind and the rain.

"Time for your diaper to be changed?" Hickok yelled back.

Tab scowled. "You think you're funny, don't you?"

"Not as funny as your face!" Hickok retorted.

Tab didn't appreciate the insult one bit. He brandished the carving knife menacingly. "You won't be such a smart aleck when we're done with you!"

"You'll get yours!" Hickok vowed.

Tab motioned with the knife, and the chicken walked off to the left, to the post where the rope was secured.

"I hope this hurts!" Tab taunted the Warrior. He looked at the second cannibal. "Go ahead!"

The chicken raised his right arm, then arced the axe downward, slicing the rope.

Ordinarily a fall of three feet wouldn't have fazed the gunman. But he had been hanging from the rope for hours; his shoulders were aching terribly, and his arms were numb from his elbows to his fingernails. He landed in the dirt, dropping to his knees, his shoulders lancing with pain.

Tab cackled. "You ain't so high and mighty now, are you?"

Hickok doubled over, feigning extreme anguish, forcing his fingers to clench and unclench.

"On your feet!" Tab ordered.

Hickok stayed put, clenching and unclenching, clenching and unclenching, feeling his forearms start to tingle.

"On your feet!" Tab commanded angrily.

Hickok glanced up, careful to keep his hands hidden by his body. "I can't! You'll have to carry me!"

Tab laughed. "We ain't going to carry your ass! On your feet! Now!"

The second cannibal stepped up to the Warrior.

Tab waved the carving knife in a small circle. "I'm not standing out in this rain all night! If you don't get up, I'll start cutting on you right here!"

Hickok pretended to rise, then slumped down again, furiously working his fingers. He couldn't go for the Colts. Too noisy.

"Enough of this bullshit!" Tab bellowed. He looked at the duck. "Bring him!"

The second cannibal stooped over, taking hold of the Warrior's left arm.

Hickok could feel sensation in his fingers again. He grinned, slowly rising, his blue eyes darting from the carving knife to the axe, assessing the probabilities, and he opted for the knife because Tab was holding it so carelessly, so loosely.

"Now that's more like it!" Tab declared, the last words he was ever to utter.

Hickok lunged, his fingers closing on the top of the carving knife blade and wrenching it from Tab's grasp even as his left leg drove up and out, catching the chicken in the midsection and sending the cannibal tumbling backwards. He slid his hands along the blade to the hilt and reversed the grip, extending the carving edge, all in a swift, smooth motion.

Tab went for the Colts.

Hickok slashed the carving knife in a vicious semicircle, and at the apex of his swing the cutting edge ripped the cannibal's throat open from one side to the other.

Tab voiced a gurgling screech, clutching his neck, blood spurting everywhere.

There was no time to finish Tab off. Hickok whirled to confront his other opponent.

The bird had regained his balance and was hurtling toward the Warrior with his axe upraised for a death blow.

Hickok backpedaled, knowing his carving knife couldn't withstand the axe, but as he retreated his moccasins slipped on the drenched, slippery ground and he fell to one knee. The movement saved his life.

The chicken had aimed a terrific swipe of the axe at the Warrior's head, but the gunman's misstep dropped him below the swinging axe.

Hickok found himself on his left knee, within arm's reach of the chicken's legs. He took instant advantage of the situation, stabbing the carving knife up and in, imbedding the blade in the bird's groin.

The second cannibal shrieked and released the axe, bending over and grabbing for his genitals.

Hickok yanked the knife out, then rose, bringing the carving knife up with the tip held vertically, savagely ramming the blade into the chicken's neck.

The chicken squawked and frantically clawed at the Warrior's eyes.

Hickok pulled the knife loose and sidestepped.

The chicken stumbled, almost straightened, then pitched onto his bill on the muddy turf.

Hickok twirled.

Tab was still on his feet, lurching toward the barracks, weaving and tottering, not ten feet off.

Hickok raced in pursuit and caught the cannibal by the scruff of the neck. He tugged, drawing Tab backwards, tripping the cannibal with his right leg.

Tab fell onto his back, the blood pouring from his throat, whining plaintively.

Hickok went to his knees, plunging the carving knife into Tab's right eye.

Tab's left eye widened and he opened his mouth to scream, but nothing came out. His arms flapping, he began convulsing uncontrollably.

Hickok maintained his pressure on the hilt until Tab's spasms ceased. He took a deep breath, then glanced at the barracks to see if more cannibals were after him.

None were in evidence.

Hickok quickly reversed his grip on the knife and applied the edge to the rope binding his wrists. Fifteen feet of rope trailed from his arms along the ground. He was lucky he hadn't become entangled during the fight! And he was fortunate the howling wind and the pummeling rain had prevented the cannibals in the barracks from hearing the struggle!

After a minute the rope parted.

Hickok's hands flashed to his Pythons, and he raised

them aloft with a smile of exultation. The feel of the pearl grips against his palms sent a surge of adrenaline coursing through his body. He stood, the wind whipping his blond hair, the rain battering his buckskins, but he ignored the storm as he faced the barracks.

So they were going to eat him for supper, were they?

Gut him like a fish and fry his flesh in a skillet!

Hickok grinned, tingling with expectation. It was time to settle accounts, to avenge the countless nameless victims of the cannibals over the years, to teach these vermin the meaning of the word justice. He holstered his Colts and stalked toward the barracks, calculating the odds. Eight cannibals had jumped him at the dock, but others had been waiting at the fort when he was brought there. Fourteen all told. Four were women, four were kids. He wasn't partial to blowing away ladyfolk and young'uns, so he'd let them live if they didn't intervene. But the male cannibals were going to meet their Maker. Tab and the bird were dead, which left eight.

The fight would be about even.

The gunman stopped outside the barracks door and checked his Pythons. Both were loaded with five rounds in the cylinder. He replaced them in their holsters, squared his shoulders, and knocked on the door.

The barracks building was a low, squat affair with a single door on the north end. The flicker of a lantern was visible through one of the two drape-covered curtains. Laughter and boisterous gab emanated from inside.

Hickok knocked once more.

"Who's there?" called a gruff voice.

Hickok recalled an ancient custom Plato had told him about when he was a small boy. In the prewar society, one night a year, the parents had sent their children out to collect as many bags of sweets as they could, simply so the parents could spend the next eleven months taking their youngsters to the dentist where the kids could have their sugar-corroded teeth repaired. A very strange custom.

"Who the hell is it?" the gruff voice demanded. "Tab? Is that you?"

"Trick or treat," Hickok declared.

"What?"

ANAHEIM RUN

"Trick or treat! Are you hard of hearing, you numb-skull?"

"Tab, you and your stupid tricks . . ." the man began as the door opened.

"How'd you guess?" Hickok said.

The cannibal, a stocky man with unkempt hair and greasy clothing, armed with a revolver angled under his deer-hide belt, gaped at the Warrior. "You!" he blurted, trying to draw.

There was no contest.

Hickok's arms were nearly invisible blurs as he pulled his irons, and the cannibal hadn't even touched his firearm when the right Colt boomed and a crimson cavity blossomed in the cannibal's forehead.

The stocky cannibal was hurled backward by the impact, crashing over a chair and smacking onto the hardwood floor.

Seven to go.

Hickok calmly stepped into the barracks, looking to the left and the right, finding cannibals on both sides.

A lean man grabbed a makeshift spear from the top of a wooden table and swept his arm back for the throw.

Hickok fired his left Python.

The spearman was hit in the nose, his head snapping backward as he was flung against the far wall.

Six left.

Pax and two other men were standing next to a row of beds aligned along the west wall. Pax's Ruger was on the nearest bed and he made a lunge for the rifle.

One of the women was screaming.

Hickok sent a slug into Pax's head and saw the chief cannibal drop like a plummeting rock. The gunfighter advanced toward the beds, his Pythons thundering twice more and the other two cannibals shared Pax's fate.

Three men remaining.

Hickok felt a tug on his left sleeve as a gunshot sounded to his rear. He whirled, discovering a male cannibal with a derringer. His right Colt cracked and bucked, dispatching the man into eternity.

Two.

"Die, you bastard!" someone shouted to his right.

The gunfighter swiveled, Pythons leveled, and there were the two men charging toward him, one armed with a short sword, the other with a knife. The left Python blasted twice.

The pair of cannibals died side by side.

Hickok grinned. And that was that!

Not quite.

There was an inarticulate scream of sheer rage from behind him.

The gunfighter spun, finding a female cannibal in a grimy brown dress three paces away with a meat cleaver waving above her head. He shot her squarely between her green eyes and she pitched onto her face at his feet.

A sudden hush descended on the barracks.

Hickok surveyed the room, recounting the bodies. The four kids and the three surviving women were huddled in the southwest corner of the barracks, their features reflecting their abject fear. He took several steps in their direction. "If I were you," he advised, "I'd stay put. Don't leave this building. I'm going to tell the Free State Army about you, and they'll most likely send a squad over here to tidy up this mess. Don't worry none. No harm will come to you. I'll see to it, personal-like." He paused, wondering if he was being understood. "You've got to stop livin' like animals. You've got to stop treatin' folks like portable munchies. The Free State people will help you. I'm sure of it. So don't skedaddle."

None of them said a word.

Hickok walked to the door, double-checking all the corpses as he went. Satisfied they were dead, he halted and reloaded the spent rounds in his Pythons. He chuckled, feeling happy and content and so . . . so alive! Reluctant as he was to admit the fact, the shootout had been just what he needed. Missing that sniper at the airport had rattled him, shaken his self-confidence. And subsequent events had only compounded the problem. But now he had redeemed himself in his eyes, had reaffirmed his prowess as a Warrior. Which meant he had to settle one more account, and pronto.

With the Gild.

The Colts reloaded, Hickok twirled them into their holsters, smiled and winked at the petrified cannibals in the corner, and ambled from the barracks into the blustering storm.

Chapter Eighteen

When the rain came, Boone was grateful.

The tempest would hide him from the . . . thing . . . in the lake.

Boone had never spent such nerve-racking hours in his entire life. After the reptillian back had appeared above the surface of the pool, he had stayed as motionless as a stone, dreading the consequences if he should move and attract the creature's attention. Eventually the mutant had submerged, and Boone had immediately gone to work on the cord binding his wrists and ankles, striving to loosen his hands or free his feet. But Nightshade's knots were too tight and the leather cord was stretched taut. Every attempt to break his bonds resulted in severe pain in his shoulders and legs. He couldn't pull on one without hurting the other.

Twice the broad brown back had crested the top of the water, floated or meandered about the pool for a spell, and then disappeared.

Boone had froze each time the creature became visible, then resumed his escape efforts once the thing submerged. But now, with the storm at full fury, he threw caution to the yowling wind and strained on the cord, hoping the elements would obscure his movements from the mutant. He recalled Kraken mentioning something about feeding someone else to the thing earlier, and he speculated on whether the mutant's full stomach had saved his life.

So far.

The Cavalryman was saturated to his skin by the rain. As the rainstorm continued, he realized his wrists were becoming more and more slippery. And was his imagination playing games, or was the leather cord developing some slack? He worked his hands back and forth, the cord digging into the skin, mixing his blood with the rain.

What was that?

Boone glanced at the pool, squinting, striving to pierce the murky gloom.

There it was again.

A deep, guttural grunt.

Boone perceived the vague outline of a huge form in the middle of the pool, and with a start he realized the thing's head was above the water *and looking in his direction!*

The mutant grunted again.

Could it see him? Would it come after him? The thought of gleaming fangs sinking into his body goaded him to action. If he could put some distance between the pool and himself! Boone dug his chin into the ground, tensed his shoulders, arched his back, and drew his knees upward, then straightened as far as the cord would allow. Resembling a buckskin clad snail, he slowly, painstakingly inched his way up the gradually curving bank. Once he slipped and his face plowed into a puddle, mud splattering his lips and cheeks. He girded his strength and kept crawling.

A tremendous splash sounded from the pool.

Boone refused to admit defeat. Expecting to feel a heavy weight crash onto his back at any moment, he snaked onward, ever upward, continuing to try to stretch the cord around his wrists even as he proceeded inch by muddy, soaked inch. He tasted the muck in his mouth and swallowed. To his astonishment, he reached the rim of the bank unmolested. His exertion was taking its toll; every muscle ached and his wrists were throbbing. But he could move his hands a bit, and thus encouraged, he struggled anew. The rain was softening the leather cord, rendering the leather more pliable.

There was a thump and a hiss from behind him.

The mutant was emerging from the pool!

Boone twisted, rolling onto his left side, desperately wrenching on the cord.

A gargantuan bulk loomed at the edge of the water.

No!

Not when he was this close!

Boone gritted his teeth, frantically rubbing his hands front and back, front and back, disregarding the throbbing anguish in his wrists. The cord was loosening more and more with every second.

But the mutant was shuffling toward him!

Boone felt the cord give way, sliding over his knuckles. He desperately tried to unravel his fingers from the entwining cord.

And then the mutant was there, a colossal reptilian monstrosity rearing skyward in the storm, the heavy downpour veiling its hideous face. The creature roared.

Boone saw the mutant's head lowering, and he caught a glimpse of a lengthy tapered snout, a mouth filled with wicked teeth, and a pair of bulging eyes. Fetid breath was on his face, almost gagging him, and he knew his doom was imminent. "No!" he shouted in defiance, wrenching on his arms one final time, and then his hands were free, and with the accomplishment came instantaneous action. He slid onto his back, drawing the Hombres faster than he had ever drawn them before, and he fired both revolvers when the mutant's mouth was widening for a bite.

A rumbling bellow greeted the gunshots.

Boone fired again as the mutant reared upright, the 44 Magnums belching their deadly lead. He blasted both guns a third time as the creature snarled and seemed to crouch at his feet, and he kept squeezing the triggers, firing as the mutant shambled toward the pool and yet again as the creature plunged into the water. Was it gone? Was it really gone? He trained the barrels on the pond, waiting for the thing to reappear.

The storm was still in full swing.

Boone sat up, grinning, scarcely able to believe he was alive. He placed the Hombres next to his feet and hurriedly freed his ankles. As he scooped the Magnums up, he stood, but a wavve of dizziness almost toppled him to his knees. He shook his head, stumbling away from the pool. Shelter! He needed shelter! Somewhere he could rest and recover his strength.

The building 40 yards off was promising.

The Cavalryman recollected Kraken saying the assassins

were going to move to another part of the park. The nearby buildings should be safe. But what if the Gild members hadn't moved yet? What if they had overheard the shots? He stopped and squatted, carefully reloading his Hombres, watching the building. Should he rest or head for the hotel? His wobbly legs served as his answer when he straightened. Rest was his first priority. He moved in the dirction of the building, his Magnums cocked, his feet squishing with every step.

A shadowy figure materialized ahead, lurking near the structure.

Boone crouched, watching the figure.

Whoever it was walked from the east to the west, an indistinct profile blurred by the torrential rain. The shape went out of sight around the west end of the building.

Boone compelled his legs to function as he hastened after the figure. A captured Gild member would be an invaluable source of information! If he could get the drop on the assassin, he'd take the S.O.B. back to Blade. Finding Hickok would have to wait. He cautiously approached the building and peeked past the northwest corner.

The figure was heading for the first structure, the one farthest south.

Hunched over, Boone crept after his quarry.

The man halted at a porch on the west side of the first building, hesitated for several moments, then walked inside.

This might be his chance! Boone hurried as quickly as he could, hoping to ambush the figure when the man emerged from the building. He attained the porch safely and stealthily climbed the wooden steps.

The interior of the building was cloaked in darkness.

Boone positioned himself to the right of the door. He holstered his left Hombre and tensed, waiting.

There was a thud from inside the building, close to the door, as if someone had bumped into a piece of furniture.

Boone glanced down at his right Hombre, debating whether he should use the barrel or the butt, and in the instant his attention was distracted from the doorway the figure appeared.

The man was looking to the north, away from Boone.

The Cavalryman reacted automatically, pouncing and wrapping his left arm around the figure's neck even as he raised his right Hombre to deliver a smashing blow to the head. Only the blow never landed.

The assassin's reflexes were uncanny. As Boone's arm clamped on his throat, he bent over at the waist and twisted his left shoulder.

Before he quite knew what was happening, Boone was airborne, flying over the assassin's shoulders and tumbling head over heels down the porch. He slammed into the ground on his stomach, temporarily dazed, but he managed to heave to his hands and knees, knowing he was dead if he didn't get up.

A hard object was suddenly pressed against the back of his head, and there was the sharp click of a hammer being cocked.

"Say your prayers, you polecat!"

Chapter Nineteen

Blade and Gallagher were questioning Frank Ebert in the privacy of Room 212 when there was a knock on the door and Bear poked his head inside.

"What is it?" Blade asked.

"They want to see the general and you in the conference room," Bear said.

"What about?"

Bear shrugged. "Beats me, bro."

Blade noticed General Gallagher was grinning. "Do you know what's going on?"

"Who, me?" Gallagher responded innocently.

Blade looked at Bear. "Will you stay here with Ebert until I return?"

"No problem," Bear replied, coming into the room.

Blade exited 212 and headed for the elevator, the general walking to his left.

"I wonder why they want us," Gallagher commented, smiling.

"You know what this is all about, don't you?" Blade demanded.

"Nope," Gallagher replied, shaking his head.

"You don't lie very well," Blade remarked.

General Gallagher laughed.

They took the elevator to the ground floor, then crossed the lobby to the conference room. The two Flathead Indians, Red Cloud and Lone Bear, were on guard. Red Cloud nodded at Blade and opened the door.

The Freedom Federation leaders and Governor Melnick were seated at a large circular table in the center of the conference room. Plato was on the far side, facing the doorway. To his right sat Kilrane, the Cavalry leader, then Zahner, the head of the Clan. Star was next, followed by the haughty Mole, Wolfe. Then came President Toland, while Governor Melnick was seated on Plato's left.

"Come in," Plato greeted them.

Blade entered, the general on his heels.

Red Cloud closed the door.

"You wanted to see us?" Blade mentioned.

"Yes," Plato said. "Governor Melnick has made an interesting proposal, one involving the entire Federation." He paused, his blue eyes studying his protégé. "One possibly involving you."

"What do you mean?" Blade queried.

Governor Melnick cleared his throat. "Perhaps, since this was my idea, I should explain the concept and the ramifications."

"Be my guest," Plato said.

Governor Melnick sat back in his plush chair. "Although I won't be making the formal public announcement until tomorrow night at the banquet, everyone in this room already knows that California will become a member of the Freedom Federation."

General Gallagher frowned.

Governor Melnick observed the general's expression. "Not everyone agrees with my decision, but I believe the years ahead will validate my judgment. As we all know, change is inevitable. Nothing ever stays the same. Either we adjust to the constant changes and grow, or we refuse to accept them and stagnate." He deliberately stared at General Gallagher. "The face of the world is changing from day to day. Slowly but surely we are recovering from the awesome destructiveness of World War Three. We must cope with dangers the prewar society never encountered. A polluted environment. Mutants, both bestial and humanoid. And there are organized threats to our existence as well, threats from those who would conquer the globe in their insane quest for domination. Enemies like the Soviets in the east, the Technics in Chicago, and the Androxians in Houston. Those are the ones we know of. Who can tell how many more enemies may be out there somewhere, awaiting their opportunity to attack?"

Blade noticed every eye in the conference room was fixed on him, as if they were gauging his reaction to Melnick's speech.

"As allies in the Freedom Federation," Governor Melnick went on, "we will be ready to band together should any one of us be besieged. We will stand united against any invader. Whether it's the Russians, the Technics, or the Androxians, they will know that to launch an assault upon any one Federation member will incur the wrath of the entire Federation."

Blade's forehead creased as he speculated on what all of this had to do with him. He stared out one of the two windows at the storm.

Melnick scanned the room. "Our policy of mutual defense will deter anyone from declaring war on us. Our treaty should serve to deter any aggression on a widespread scale. But what about isolated incidents? What about localized problems within the boundaries of each Federation member? The Civilized Zone, the Cavalry, the Flathead Indians all control extensive areas, and trouble spots arise from time to time within the boundaries of each. The Cavalry has been unable to solve a series of mysterious disappearances. And the Flatheads have been raided by the Bear People from Idaho. Neither of these episodes justify massing the military might of the Federation, yet each has posed a major problem for the respective Federation members involved."

Blade was beginning to understand why Melnick was a politician. The man could talk rings around a tree.

"I consider California to be honored at being admitted into the Federation," the governor was saying. "I wanted to show my gratitude somehow, and after due deliberation I hit on a practical idea." He looked at Blade. "And this is where you come in."

"How so?" Blade inquired.

"I propose establishing a special strike force," Melnick explained.

"A strike force?" Blade repeated quizzically.

"Yes. A mobile force organized with one purpose in mind. Namely, to deal with just such trouble spots as we've been discussing. If a localized problem develops anywhere within the Freedom Federation, or outside our boundaries for that matter, this strike force will be dispatched to deal with the situation. Any request for aid from a Federation member will be sufficient to have the strike force sent out immediately," Governor Melnick elaborated.

"The idea is commendable," Blade commented. "But there are drawbacks."

"Such as what?" Melnick asked.

"The Freedom Federation members are scattered over the western half of what was once the U.S.," Blade said. "Considerable distances are involved. Where is this strike force going to be based?"

"Right here in Los Angeles," Melnick said.

"Okay. Do you realize how long it would take this strike force to reach the Flatheads from here? Or the Dakota territory? Overland travel is extremely hazardous and very time-consuming. Weeks could elapse between the request for aid and the arrival of the strike force," Blade stated.

"Using conventional vehicles, yes," Melnick concurred, then smiled. "But not if we use the VTOL's."

"Your jets?" Blade queried.

Governor Melnick nodded. "Their vertical take off and landing capability make them ideal for our purpose. They could transport the strike force anywhere in the Freedom Federation, or the Outlands, within a span of hours."

"They could," Blade admitted.

"By the same token," Melnick detailed, "if we set up a weekly shuttle service for the VTOL's to carry messages back and forth, we can insure requests for aid are relayed relatively promptly."

"It sounds to me like you've thought of everything," Blade complimented the governor. "But I don't see what all of this has to do with me."

Melnick glanced at Plato.

Plato gazed around the table, then at Blade. "We have been discussing the organizational requirements for the strike force," he said slowly, "and we have reached agreement on the best method."

"You're going to use soldiers from California," Blade guessed.

"No," Plato said. "We have another idea."

"What is it?" Blade probed.

"We believe the best method entails having the strike

ANAHEIM RUN

force comprised of seven members," Plato revealed. "One from each Federation faction."

"One from each?" Blade said, and suddenly he saw where the conversation was leading. A tight sensation developed in his gut.

"Precisely," Plato confirmed. "Each Federation member will volunteer one person to become part of the strike force. We have decided, by the way, to call this strike force the Freedom Force."

"And you say you're going to call for volunteers?" Blade asked.

Plato nodded. "Our idea is to have each volunteer serve in the Freedom Force for a period of one year. Volunteers would be rotated annually."

Blade relaxed a bit. "Sounds great to me."

"I was hoping you would say that," Plato said. "Because by the unanimous concensus of all the leaders, we would like you to volunteer to head the Freedom Force."

Blade had seen the request coming, but he was still stunned. "Me?" he blurted out.

"You," Plato reiterated. "You would be responsible for training the seven members of the Freedom Force and shaping them into a cohesive fighting unit. General Gallagher would be your liaison with Governor Melnick."

"Gallagher?" Blade glanced at the general.

General Gallagher nodded, grinning impishly. "Surprised, huh?"

"I thought you didn't like the treaty," Blade mentioned. "Why would you want to get involved with the Freedom Force?"

"I don't like the damn treaty," Gallagher stated, "but I've agreed to give the treaty a chance."

"And General Gallagher is a good soldier," Governor Melnick interjected. "He follows orders, whether he likes the orders or not. And he always performs one hundred percent."

Blade looked at Plato. "But why me? There must be dozens of equally qualified candidates to head the Freedom Force!"

"Name one," Plato said.

"Hickok," Blade suggested.

"Too impetuous," Plato remarked.

"Then how about Rikki, or Yama, or Spartacus," Blade said, mentioning other Warriors. "Or someone from the Cavalry, like Boone? Or an officer from the Civilized Zone Army? Or General Gallagher himself?"

"Not one of them has your experience," Plato stated. "Not one of them is as ideally suited for the task."

"But what about the Warriors? Who would be in charge of them during the year I'm away?" Blade asked.

"The Family Elders will select a temporary head Warrior," Plato replied. "Someone to fill in while you are gone."

"A year is too long," Blade objected. "I won't stay away from my family for that long."

"And you wouldn't be," Plato mentioned. "Governor Melnick will fly your wife and son out here. Jenny and little Gabe will live in L.A. with you."

Blade fell silent, emotionally shocked. Leave the Family? Leave the Home? Live in California for a year! All his truest friends and loved ones were in Minnesota.

Plato rose and walked around the table to Blade. "I'm sorry," he apologized softly. "If there was anyone else as competent as you, I wouldn't be making this appeal. We all feel your presence is essential to the Freedom Force's success. You have traveled extensively throughout the country, and you have firsthand experience with our enemies. Whether you like it or not, you are famous. You have acquired a reputation as a fighter, a man not to be trifled with. This reputation would work in your favor in your new capacity."

Blade stared at the floor. "I just don't know," he said bleakly. "I don't want to leave the Home."

Plato's features saddened. "And I don't want to see you leave. You are like a son to me." He paused and sighed. "You have served the Family nobly as the head Warrior for almost a decade. Now you have an opportunity to serve the Freedom Federation on a much broader scale. Untold millions will benefit from your work. All I ask is that you give the matter serious deliberation."

Blade looked up. "How soon do you want my answer?"

"As promptly as possible," Plato replied.

"I need to be alone," Blade said. He wheeled and stalked from the conference room, heading for the front entrance. Absorbed in his concentration, he was at the glass doors before he realized the rainstorm had not abated. Annoyed, craving solitude, he shoved the doors open and marched outside. The wind lashed his hair and the cool drops of rain peppered his face.

"Are you okay, sir?" one of the soldiers guarding the entrance inquired.

"Fine," Blade snapped. He bore to the left, following the sidewalk, his inner feelings matching nature's onslaught. How could Plato ask him to do such a thing? After all they had meant to each other!

The sidewalk wound along the front of the hotel, then branched off. One path led to a parking lot on the east side of the hotel, while the other continued around the hotel to the gardens in the rear.

Blade took the branch leading to the gardens, oblivious to the inclement weather. The very notion of leaving the Family was intolerable. How would Jenny react? His wife was as attached to the Home as he was. How could he ask her to sever her roots and move to Los Angeles, even if it was for only a year?

A year!

A year without seeing Hickok or Geronimo or Joshua! A year of uncertainty, a year of one deadly mission after another. Was it fair to subject his wife and son to such a strain, never knowing if he would return from the latest assignment? He never had liked leaving the Home on extended runs in the SEAL. Every moment he was away from Jenny and Gabe caused him anguish.

The wind was howling like a banshee.

Blade stopped and gazed skyward, closing his eyes, letting the rain pelt him. Dear Spirit! What should he do? Was he really essential to the operation of the Freedom Force? Plato must be mistaken. Surely Rikki-Tikki-Tavi could handle the job. Or Yama. He opened his eyes, gazing absently at the landscape, buffeted by the gusts.

Someone was approaching from the direction of the gardens.

Blade distinguished the forms of four soaked soldiers coming his way. They were advancing in single file, evidently patrolling the grounds. He stepped to one side so they could pass.

The trooper in the front spotted the Warrior and seemed to hesitate for an instant, then proceeded. "I didn't expect to find anyone out here," he remarked when he was two yards off.

"I needed some fresh air," Blade said.

The soldier grinned. "Nice night for a stroll."

Blade, hands on his hips, chuckled. "You've got that right."

"Be seeing you," the soldier said.

Blade idly watched the four pass him. He didn't envy them. Spending hours patrolling the grounds in this weather would be sheer drudgery. Their drenched uniforms were plastered to their bodies. Two of them tucked their chins into their chests as they passed him, futilely endeavoring to keep the rain from their faces. Their weapons were slung over their right shoulders and partially protected by their arms. Even the hair protruding from under the helmets of two of them was slick with water.

Blade saw them round the corner and head toward the front entrance. He hoped they were due for relief. Shrugging, he resumed his walk.

Now where was he?

Oh, yes. There had to be someone else capable of heading the Freedom Force. Rikki-Tikki-Tavi was the Family's supreme martial artist. If anyone was competent, Rikki was. And Yama was one of the deadliest Warriors. True, Yama had never held a position of leadership, but he was thoroughly reliable in every respect.

There was a loud snap to the right as a tree limb broke and fell to the ground.

Blade walked to the rear of the hotel and surveyed the gardens, his mind a confused jumble of disturbed thoughts. His ambivalence was distressing. If he told the leaders no, what would they do? Select someone else? Abandon the idea? Would they hold his refusal against him? How he wished he was back at the Home, in bed with

Jenny in their cabin, snuggling with her and forgetting all the cares in the world! He became lost in thought, strolling for another 20 yards.

His right boot bumped something.

Blade halted and glanced down, his eyes taking a second to identify the inky form at his feet as that of a soldier.

The trooper was flat on his back.

Blade knelt, feeling for a pulse in the soldier's neck. His right hand made contact with a gaping cavity in the trooper's throat. The man was dead.

The assassins must be on the hotel grounds! At least one of them!

Blade stood, his hands on his Bowies, peering into the night, searching his immediate vicinity, and suddenly he stiffened, startled, remembering the patrol he had passed just a couple of minutes ago. *The hair sticking from under the helmets of two of them had been slick with water! But the soldiers in the California army were all required to wear their hair cut short! He had not seen one with shoulder-length hair!*

The wind was singing its siren song as the Warrior raced like a madman toward the front of the hotel.

Chapter Twenty

"That was Blade, wasn't it, guv?" Charley asked as they rounded the northeast corner of the hotel and headed for the front entrance.

Kraken, in the lead, nodded.

"Why didn't we waste him, mate?" Charley inquired.

Kraken looked over his right shoulder. Charley was behind him, followed by Nightshade and Leftwich. "Because we were too close to him when we first saw him. We would have had to unsling our Darters, and his hands were almost touching those Bowies of his. Besides, he had an M-16 over his shoulder. We could have killed him, but he might have taken one or two of us with him, and we can't afford to lose a single man at this stage of the game."

Nightshade raised his left arm and pointed straight ahead.

Kraken saw them too. A pair of guards outside the front entrance. He continued moving toward the glass doors until he was 15 yards from the soldiers, then he stopped and motioned for the others to gather closer. "This is it," he told them. "We go in shooting. Stay close to me and kill everyone you see. I know the layout. The Federation leaders could be in the lobby or the conference room. They won't be hard to find."

"How many soldiers do you think are inside?" Leftwich asked.

"Perhaps two or three dozen," Kraken answered.

Leftwich whistled.

"The soldiers will not pose a problem," Kraken assured him. "Our Darters are fully loaded with thirty darts apiece. That's one hundred and twenty rounds. We can handle a few dozen inexperienced soldiers."

"Just say the word," Charley said.

Kraken started to turn, then paused. "I stand corrected.

There is one person we should avoid killing if possible."

"Who's the exception?" Leftwich inquired.

"Our employer has an undercover agent at the summit," Kraken disclosed. "A woman. Blonde. About five eight. I was provided with her description but not given her name. To play it safe, don't kill any blonde not wearing a uniform."

"Got it," Leftwich said.

"Unsling your Darters," Kraken ordered, facing the entrance and taking his rifle from his shoulder. He knew the conference room was on the ground floor, and he would have preferred to try and ambush the delegates from outside. All he would have needed to do was locate the appropriate window. But the Darters' singular deficiency had dissuaded him from the course of action. The explosive darts detonated after penetrating whatever they hit, so the first rounds fired through the window would detonate just inside the window pane, far short of the leaders, alerting them and allowing them to seek cover while the security forces came to their rescue. An ambush through the window might succeed in slaying several of the leaders, but his employer wanted all of them dead—Plato, Toland, and Melnick at the very minimum. To guarantee the success of the assignment, Kraken was compelled to take the direct approach.

A frontal assault.

Kraken flicked the safety off on his Darter. "On me," he said, and jogged toward the front entrance.

The two soldiers outside the doors were gazing at the foursome in evident perplexity. "What's up?" one of them inquired as the quartet came abreast of the entrance.

"Just this," Kraken said, and shot both of them, once each in the chest. He pushed through the glass doors, scanning the lobby. Emery had mentioned the conference room was on the right-hand side of the lobby, but had not pinpointed its exact location with reference to the front entrance. Kraken had hoped to find the Federation leaders gathered in the lobby, but instead there were about a dozen troopers and perhaps an equal number of bureaucrats. His gaze alighted on a pair of Flathead Indians standing next to a closed door, and all at once he knew.

Charley, Leftwich, and Nightshade came through the glass doors.

Some of the occupants of the lobby were staring at the four dripping newcomers in confusion.

"Kill them and follow me!" Kraken commanded, opening up with the Darter as he sprinted in the direction of the Flatheads.

Charley, Leftwich, and Nightshade began firing as rapidly as targets presented themselves.

Bedlam ensued. The Darters downed soldiers and civilians with indiscriminate abandon. Faces exploded outward, heads ruptured, and torsos were racked by the lethal darts. The silent Darters were an eerie counterpart of the confusion and clamor they generated. Men and women screamed as they died. Some of the bureaucrats attempted to flee in a screeching panic but were shot in the back of the head. Blood sprayed over the carpet and the furniture. Bodies littered the floor.

Kraken saw the two Flatheads charging toward them. He snapped off a shot, his dart catching the younger of the Indians in the head. The older Flathead stopped and fired his M-16, and Kraken heard someone grunt behind him. He sent a dart into the second Flathead's face, and the Indian's nose and forehead erupted like a miniature volcano. Kraken looked over his left shoulder.

Charley had been creased on the left side of his head. His curly hair was matted with blood. He grinned and hefted his Darter. "Just a scratch, mate!"

Kraken headed for the conference room door just as a dozen more troopers appeared at the rear of the lobby and surged forward. The assassins concentrated their fire on this new threat, blowing apart soldier after soldier. A few of the troopers managed to return the withering barrage, but their shots were wild and ineffective. In the space of seconds all of the soldiers were dead or writhing on the floor in their death throes.

An elevator door opened on the left side of the lobby, disgorging three men. One was a diminutive frontiersman in buckskins, armed with a Winchester. The second was a man with a beard, dressed all in black, carrying an M-16. The third was a nondescript type, also holding an M-16.

Three of the Federation delegates! "There!" Kraken shouted, swiveling and shooting.

Charley, Leftwich, and Nightshade did likewise.

The nondescript delegate was the first to fall, half of his face splattering the carpet.

The bearded one in black toppled over next.

Undaunted, the feisty frontiersman kept coming, levering the rounds into his Winchester and coolly sighting before squeezing the trigger.

Leftwich was knocked backward by the impact of a slug striking his right shoulder, but he retained his footing.

Kraken and Nightshade fired simultaneously, and the frontiersman flipped onto the floor, convulsing.

"Did it penetrate your vest?" Kraken asked Leftwich.

Leftwich shook his head.

"That door!" Kraken yelled, pointing at the conference room. "Kill everyone inside!" He raced toward the door, confident of success. No more soldiers had appeared. Nothing stood between them and the completion of their assignment!

But Kraken was wrong.

Two men burst through a door at the rear of the lobby, on the right side. Both men wore buckskins, and both were armed with a pair of revolvers. One was blonde with a moustache, the other had long brown hair and was cleanshaven. Both wore the determined expressions of men out for revenge.

Hickok and Boone!

"Take cover!" Kraken bellowed, diving behind a sofa. He knew better than to expose himself to the two pistoleers. Their reputations as shootists were well deserved.

Nightshade ducked in the shelter of a large mahogany chair.

But Charley and Leftwich foolishly charged the gunfighters, prompted by their desire to resolve the conflict quickly, both believing their marksmanship equal to the occasion.

Kraken happened to look to the rear, and his eyes widened as he saw Blade barreling through the front doors. The Gild had lost the initiative. Fulfilling the contract was no longer feasible. Surviving was the issue. Surviving to try again another day. Both the front and the rear were blocked by exceptionally skilled adversaries, and reinforcements might arrive at any moment. There was one recourse open, and that was to retreat.

The elevator door was still open.

"Follow me!" Kraken shouted, dashing toward the left side of the lobby, keeping doubled over, weaving among the furniture.

Nightshade kept pace with his chief.

Kraken reached the elevator and scooted inside, glancing back and seeing Hickok down Leftwich with two shots to the head even as Boone's Hombres thundered and Charley was captapulted into a potted plant.

Blade, his M-16 in his hands, was racing on a course to the elevator.

Kraken punched the button for the first floor as Nightshade slid inside. The elevator doors shut and the car began climbing. He realized Blade would be in hot pursuit, and Kraken grinned as his fertile mind concocted an escape plan. What was the room his employer's secret agent was in? Room 103! That was it!

Nightshade motioned with his hands.

"We're not out of the woods yet," Kraken agreed. "But I can get us both out of here if you'll buy me the time I need."

Nightshade grimly nodded.

"Good. Here's what I want you to do . . . ."

Chapter Twenty-One

Blade was 20 feet from the elevator when the doors closed and it ascended. Fuming, he sped up to the elevator, watching the numeral display overhead.

"Wait for us, pard!"

Blade looked to his rear, smiling at the sight of Hickok and Boone running his way.

The elevator stopped on the first floor.

"Did those bastards take the elevator?" Hickok queried as he reached his friend.

Blade nodded, staring at Boone. "I want you to stay here in case they get past us."

"They won't get past me," Boone vowed.

Blade stabbed the down button, impatiently waiting while the elevator descended to the lobby. He stepped inside before the doors were fully open, Hickok right behind him.

"I have a score to settle," the gunman announced.

Blade pressed the button for the first floor. "I was worried about you," he remarked.

The elevator doors closed and it started upward.

"They might be waitin' for us," Hickok said.

"Let them!" Blade stated gruffly, gripping his M-16, facing the doors.

"I missed you, big guy," Hickok mentioned.

"Where were you?" Blade asked, his gaze riveted on the indicator panel.

"Takin' lessons in culinary etiquette," Hickok replied.

Before Blade could comment, the elevator coasted to a stop and the doors widened.

Hickok exited first, his Pythons held close to his hips, surveying the corridor. No one was in the hall and all of the doors in sight were closed. "Is there a back way out of here? A stairwell?" he whispered.

"I don't know," Blade said, advancing along the left wall. "I don't think so."

Hickok took the right side. "I won't rest until I've nailed Kraken and his mutant buddy, Nightshade."

"You know who they were?" Blade queried in a hushed tone.

"The lowest scum alive," Hickok responded. "But not for long, if I can help it."

The Warriors lapsed into silence as they neared the first door, Room 101 on the right side of the hall. Blade trained his M-16 on the door while Hickok tried the knob. The door opened and the gunman vanished into the room, reappearing moments later shaking his head. They cautiously proceeded to the next door, Room 102 on the left. This time Hickok covered Blade as the giant Warrior, without bothering to check if the door was locked, drew his right leg up, then kicked. The wood near the doorknob splintered with a resounding crash and the door swiveled inward. Blade vaulted into the room, his finger on the trigger of his M-16, but the room was empty. He stooped to peer under the bed and verified no one was secreted in the bathroom or the closet.

"Where the blazes are they?" Hickok hissed as his towering companion emerged from the room.

Blade shook his head and kept going.

The next room was 103, on the right side of the hall. The two Warriors were a yard from the door when it unexpectedly opened and a woman stepped into the corridor, a sandy-haired blonde in a red dress and jacket. Her brown eyes seemed to register surprise at the sight of them.

"What was that noise I just heard?" she asked Blade, closing her door.

"Do you know her?" Hickok inquired.

"This is Melissa Parmalee," Blade said, introducing her. "One of President Toland's assistants."

"Howdy, ma'am," Hickok said. "We're lookin' for a couple of varmints. Have you seem 'em?"

"What are you talking about?" Parmalee queried.

"We're searching for a pair of assassins," Blade explained.

"Assassins? Here?" Paramelee said doubtfully.

"Didn't you hear the ruckus in the lobby?" Hickok questioned.

"I haven't heard a thing until just now," Parmalee answered. "I've been taking a nap. I have a headache, and President Toland said I wasn't needed for a while."

"So you didn't see anyone?" Blade asked.

Parmalee shook her head.

Hickok started to walk past her toward her door.

"Where are you going?" Parmalee demanded, grabbing his left arm.

"To check your room," Hickok told her, staring at the hand on his forearm.

"That won't be necessary," Parmalee stated. "There's no one in my room."

"Then you won't mind if we check, will you?" Hickok rejoined.

"Really. It isn't necessary," Parmalee reiterated, looking at Blade, smiling sweetly. "Tell him."

"Check the room," Blade ordered.

Hickok pulled his arm from Parmalee's grasp and reached for the doorknob, keeping his eyes on her, suspicious of her behavior. He detected motion out of the corner of his right eye and spun.

The door had been yanked wide, framing Nightshade in the doorway, his Darter in his left hand, the barrel pointing upward, mere inches from the gunman.

Hickok, his Colts at waist level, knowing there wasn't time to tilt the barrels for a head shot, planted two shots in the mutant's chest.

Nightshade was rocked by the impact of the slugs, but he only stumbled backward a step, then furiously surged forward, his right hand closing on the Darter barrel.

Hickok fired both Pythons again, astonished when his shots failed to drop the mutant.

Nightshade clubbed the amazed Warrior on the head with his rifle butt, his prodigious power sending the gunman flying across the corridor into the far wall.

Hickok slumped to the floor, his Colts sliding from his hands, his eyes closed.

Blade, unable to shoot because Hickok had blocked his line of fire, now aimed at the mutant. But before he could squeeze the trigger, intervention from an unforeseen source turned the tide of battle.

Melissa Parmalee—shapely, slim, five feet eight and dainty—grabbed the M-16 barrel and *tore the gun from his hands!* The M-16 went off, but the round imbedded harmlessly in the ceiling.

Blade crouched, his hands gripping his Bowies, his astounded gaze on Parmalee.

The woman tilted her head and laughed, a brittle, malevolent titter. "Look at him!" she said to Nightshade. "The fool can't believe his eyes!"

Nightshade grinned and pointed his Darter at the Warrior.

"No!" Parmalee exclaimed. "He's mine! This will only take a minute. I want the privilege of snapping his spine! No one else is on this floor. You watch the elevator."

Nightshade nodded.

Parmalee disdainfully extended the M-16 toward Blade. "Here! Do you want this?"

Blade waited for her to make a move.

Parmalee snickered. "I guess you don't!" She held the stock in her right hand and squeezed, crushing the gun with a grinding of metal and a crunching noise, then contemptuously flung the useless weapon to the floor.

"Have you figured it out yet?" Parmalee baited him.

"I think so," Blade responded.

"Oh, really?" Parmalee retorted sarcastically.

"I was wrong," Blade said. "The Soviets didn't hire the Gild to assassinate the Federation leaders. They don't want to kill just the leaders. The Russians want to crush the entire Federation. Their spy, Ebert, would have relayed details of the summit, and the Soviets would plan their strategy accordingly."

"But if the Soviets didn't hire the Gild," Parmalee observed mockingly, "who did?"

"I didn't know until just now when you destroyed the gun," Blade stated. "I didn't realize more than one of our enemies might have a spy planted in President Toland's administration. But the Civilized Zone is the perfect place to plant a spy. The Family, the Clan, and the Moles are too small to successfully infiltrate an outsider. And the

Flatheads and the Cavalry are out of the question, unless the spy is an Indian or an expert horseman. But the Civilized Zone is so large, with President Toland's staff numbering in the dozens, that installing a secret agent would be relatively simple."

Parmalee took a step toward the Warrior. "But you still haven't told me which side I'm with. And here I heard you were such a bright little boy!"

"Only someone with incredible strength could pulverize an M-16," Blade noted. "A mutant, say . . . or an android."

Melissa Parmalee cackled. "Excellent!"

Blade's mind flashed back to his harrowing experiences in Houston, Texas, renamed Androxia by the android rulers of that city-state. Developed by NASA prior to the war to replace human astronauts and prevent the loss of human lives, the androids had continued producing themselves after civilization crumbled to a standstill. Eventually, the androids had conquered the surviving humans in southern Texas and established themselves as the ruling class. Dubbed the Superiors, the androids were led by a computerized entity known as Primator, an entity Blade had exterminated before escaping from Androxia.

Parmalee took another step. "Now that the socializing is dispensed with, let's conclude this, shall we?"

Blade whipped his Bowies from their sheaths and backed up. "There's one thing I don't understand," he said, stalling, biding time until he could devise a scheme to dispose of the android.

"Just *one* thing?" Parmalee rejoined.

"I didn't know there were female androids," Blade mentioned. "All I saw in Androxia were male androids."

Parmalee smiled proudly. "I am the first of a new breed of Superior. Not only are my external features female in aspect, but I have been endowed with a wider range of human characteristics than my predecessors. I make the perfect spy. And once I have proven myself in the field, Primator intends to manufacture thousands more like me."

"But Primator was terminated," Blade said.

Parmalee grinned. "Did you really believe Primator was

slain by a lowly human?"

Blade straightened. "Primator is alive?"

"And he sends his regards," Parmalee declared maliciously.

"Then the hiring of the Gild wasn't merely to try and ruin the Freedom Federation," Blade deduced. "It was personal. Primator wants revenge!"

Parmalee nodded. "Finally you see the light! Preventing California from joining the Freedom Federation was a secondary goal. Eliminating the leaders was also incidental. Primator wants retribution. Employing the Gild was a means to an end." She paused. "I'm under orders not to jeopardize my clandestine status. But I was given definite instructions in case a situation like this should arise. If the opportunity arose to achieve Primator's revenge without risk of apprehension, I was directed to use my personal discretion. And guess what?"

Blade's fingers tightened on the Bowies. He expected the android to assail him and he wasn't disappointed.

Parmalee executed a flying tackle, her shoulders driving into the giant's midsection as her arms wrapped around his waist.

Blade was knocked backward, staggered by the android's super-human might, stumbling and falling onto his back with her on top bestriding his chest.

Parmalee lunged, attempting to pin the Warrior's arms to the floor.

Blade arced his right Bowie up and in, sinking the ten-inch blade into the android's chest between the breasts.

Parmalee looked at the Bowie, then backhanded the Warrior across the mouth, stunning him and dislodging his right hand from the Bowie hilt. She slowly stood and stepped backward. "We won't be needing this anymore," she announced, her right hand effortlessly pulling the Bowie from her body.

Blade rolled onto his feet, squatting, his leg muscles tensing for a spring.

Parmalee tossed the right Bowie aside.

Blade performed a tackle of his own, bearing the android to the floor, the tip of his left Bowie tearing into her abdomen. He clasped the hilt with both hands and surged, cleaving a six-inch gash in her belly and ripping her clothes.

Parmalee laughed, then rammed her right knee into the small of the Warrior's broad back, propelling him forward where she could fasten her fingers onto his throat.

Blade rose unsteadily, hampered by the android clinging to his neck. He wrenched on the left Bowie, cutting her open some more, a colorless liquid spurting from her ruptured abdomen and covering his hands and forearms. And still Parmalee clung to him, her nails digging into his throat, beginning to constrict his breathing. He was forced to release the Bowie and hammer at her with his pile-driver fists, pounding her face again and again and again. Her nose was crushed by one of his blows, flattening into a pulpy mass. He battered her mouth and her chin, splitting her lips, but his onslaught was unavailing. She simply dug her fingers in deeper. It felt like his neck was being pried apart.

Parmalee tried to kick the Warrior in the crotch.

Blade twisted, avoiding her foot. He grabbed her wrists and endeavored to pull her hands from his throat, his massive muscles bulging with his herculean effort, the veins on his temples protruding. But the android clung to him like a leech, slowly but surely strangling him.

He had to do something!

The gleam of a metallic object on the floor drew his attention, something lying near Hickok's leg.

One of the Pythons!

His breaths coming in ragged gasps, feeling as if his throat was about to be crushed at any second, in desperation he deliberately plowed into Parmalee and sent both of them toppling to the carpet with the android on the bottom. He had to act before Parmalee or the mutant guessed his intent! The android was smiling.

The Python was inches from his left hand.

Blade scooped up the Colt, jammed the barrel into Parmalee's open mouth, all the way, and squeezed the trigger twice in succession.

The android's eyes enlarged in bewilderment. Parmalee went rigid for an instant, and then shoved the Warrior from her. She sat up, vigorously shaking her head.

Blade was to the android's right, on his hands and knees, the Python in his left hand. He saw fluid flowing from under her hair, spreading over her shoulders, and he raised the Colt for another shot.

There was a slight sound to the rear, and the Warrior was delivered a brutal smash to the rear of his head.

Blade collapsed, sagging to the floor, almost unconscious, releasing the Python from his numb fingers. He realized the mutant must have clobbered him with the rifle butt, and he expected to receive a shot to the brain to finish him off. Instead, a hand gripped his right shoulder and he was savagely flipped over onto his back.

The mutant was glaring at the Warrior. He slowly began to aim the Darter.

Blade understood. Nightshade wanted him to see his demise, wanted to instill terror in his victim. But the plan backfired. Instead of feeling fright, Blade became enraged. He thought of all the bodies he'd seen in the lobby, all the needless deaths the assassins had caused, all the misery the murderers had perpetrated to satisfy the retributive craving of a vile dictator, and his fury mounted, lending strength to his limbs and clarity to his vision.

Nightshade was sneering in triumph when the Warrior's right boot lashed out and caught him in the left knee. There was a pop, and the mutant's leg buckled. He snapped off a shot, but the explosive dart missed the Warrior's head and detonated in the carpet several inches to the right.

Blade kicked with both boots, catching the mutant's right leg below the knee, and Nightshade tottered backward and fell onto his back. Blade was up and bounding forward before the mutant could recover. Nightshade was just scrambling to his knees when the Warrior delivered a kick to the mutant's chin, toppling Nightshade over and sending the rifle flying. Blade closed in, assuming the mutant was down for the count. But he underestimated his foe.

Nightshade, on his right side, his left leg out of commission with a busted kneecap, rolled to the left and struck at the Warrior with his right foot. Blade easily sidestepped, but in so doing he came within reach of Nightshade's arms, and Nightshade reached out and seized the Warrior's ankles and yanked.

Blade felt his feet slip out from under him, and then he was on the floor next to the mutant. The two of them exchanged a flurry of hand blows, neither very effective because of their awkward positions. Blade punched Nightshade on the jaw, rocking the mutant, but Nightshade immediately countered with an excruciating blow to Blade's abdomen.

Nightshade tried to apply pressure to Blade's throat, to finish the job Parmalee had started, but the Warrior knocked his arms aside.

Blade was rapidly tiring. The strain of the combat with the android and the rifle butt to the head were taking their toll. His reflexes became sluggish, and he was able to ward off fewer and fewer of the mutant's strikes.

Nightshade sensed his advantage and pressed it, grappling with the Warrior and succeeding in butting his forehead into Blade's chin. The Warrior was momentarily stunned, and Nightshade used those precious seconds to scramble erect on his good leg and hobble toward the Darter lying a few feet away.

"No you don't, gruesome!"

Nightshade turned at the sound of the stern command, and there was the gunfighter, Hickok, with his revolvers in his hands and a fierce expression on his face. Nightshade froze.

"How'd you do it?" Hickok asked.

Nightshade had no idea what the Warrior was talking about.

"You took four shots to the chest at close range," Hickok said. "How come you're still alive?"

Nightshade glanced at the Darter, measuring the distance.

"Don't even think it!" Hickok warned. "Now answer me! How come you're still alive?"

Nightshade tapped his shirt.

"What?" Hickok queried.

The assassin unbuttoned two of his shirt buttons and tugged the fabric aside, exposing the garment underneath.

Hickok's reaction was mystifying to the mutant. The

gunman did a double take, then laughed. "A bulletproof vest! You were all wearing bulletproof vests!"

Nightshade nodded.

"Then that's why that joker on the terminal roof didn't go down!" Hickok said, sounding relieved. "I didn't miss!"

Nightshade, puzzled, remained immobile.

"Thanks," Hickok declared. "I needed that." He paused. "I'm not about to plug you when you're unarmed. Unlike you, I don't kill unless it's necessary. I'll give you the chance you never would have given me."

To Nightshade's amazement, the gunman holstered his Colts.

"It's your move," Hickok said.

And move he did, with all the speed in his mutant frame. Nightshade dove for the Darter and whirled, stupefied to find the Warrior hadn't even moved. The gunfighter's hands were still by his sides!

But not for long. Hickok saw the look on Nightshade's face, saw the mutant believed he'd won. His arms a blur, Hickok punctuated the assassin's delusions with twin blasts from his Pythons.

Nightshade's head jerked backward and he was thrown onto his back by the force of the slugs. He convulsed for a moment, then was still.

Blade was slowly rising to his feet. "Thanks," he said. "I owe you."

"You don't owe me diddly," Hickok responded. "What are friends for?"

A female voice tittered. "Friends are friends and mares are does and mastodons eat poison ivy!"

Hickok swiveled to the left.

Melissa Parmalee was sitting on the floor with a remarkably stupid expression on her wreck of a face.

"What the heck!" Hickok exclaimed.

"She's an android," Blade informed him.

"An android?" Hickok stepped up to her and leaned down, studying her features.

Parmalee giggled. "Two and two is nine, and fifty and four decades make a stitch in time." She applauded her poetry.

"What the blazes is she babbling about?" Hickok asked.

"Her circuits are damaged," Blade explained. "I shot her in the head."

Parmalee beamed at Hickok. "Jack and Jill went up the hill to fetch a pail of water. Nine months later, wouldn't you know, Jill had a daughter!" She laughed uproariously.

"Shut her up," Blade ordered.

Hickok pressed the Python barrels to her eyes and squeezed the triggers.

Epilogue

Blade stood on the sidewalk outside the front entrance to the hotel, enjoying the warmth of the afternoon sun on his body. He ached all over, and swallowing was an exercise in the finer art of torture. His mind reviewed the aftermath of the assassination attempt, and he frowned. Forty-three deaths! The toll was staggering! He thought of the ones he'd known, of Lone Bear and Red Cloud, of the Mole and Brother Timothy. And Hamlin! How could he forget Hamlin? All killed in the performance of their duty. All slain needlessly, casualties of humankind's seemingly endless thirst for blood and destruction. How long would it take? he wondered. How many centuries of warfare? How many horrors would be unleashed before the people of the earth awoke to the insanity of it all? How long before there really was peace on earth and goodwill in the hearts of all men and women?

At the rate the human race was going, maybe never!

There were footsteps behind him and he turned.

Plato intently scrutinized the Warrior as he approached. "How are you feeling?" he inquired.

"I'll survive," Blade said.

"You know why I'm here," Plato stated.

Blade nodded. "They want to know my decision."

"Have you decided?" Plato asked.

Blade sighed and gazed heavenward. They were on the west side of the hotel. Far off, winging in the direction of the Pacific Ocean, was a flock of white birds. Gulls?

"If you don't want to do it, I will understand," Plato commented. "I wouldn't force you to do anything you disliked."

"You're not forcing me at all," Blade said. "And until last night, until the assassins attacked, I was ready to tell the Federation leaders to take a high dive off a low cliff. Tactfully, of course."

"Of course," Plato grinned.

"But then I got to thinking about the attack," Blade mentioned. "About all the lives lost. And I can't seem to stop thinking about it."

"You've seen death before," Plato remarked.

"Many times," Blade acknowledged. "But this was different."

"How so?"

"This episode made me realize something," Blade said. "It made me see a fact I've been avoiding for years. The Family Elders have taught us to strive for spiritual mastery in our lives. Whether we're Warriors, or Tillers, or Weavers, or whatever, we're inspired to aspire to ideals of truth and brotherhood. And within the limited confines of the Home this relative perfection is attainable. But once we're outside the Home, forget it! It's dog eat dog. The survival of the fittest. As head Warrior, my responsibility has been to make damn sure the violence outside hasn't spread inside."

"You have discharged your responsibility superbly," Plato said, complimenting him.

"I guess," Blade stated. "But I've overlooked an important fact."

"Which is?"

Blade stared at Plato. "As long as there is violence outside the Home, as long as there are degenerates and defectives and killers of every stripe out there, we will constantly be confronted with violence inside the Home."

"That should be obvious," Plato remarked.

"It was and it wasn't," Blade said. "Every time the Home was in danger, or every time I went on a run to St. Louis, or New York City, or Philadelphia, or wherever, I kept telling myself that each incident, each trip, would be the last. I deluded myself into believing the Family would never be threatened again if I could eliminate the latest menace. I hated those runs, Plato. I hated being away from the Family, from my wife and son. I would always fool myself into believing each run was the final one." He laughed. "What an idiot!"

"You're being too hard on yourself," Plato opined.

"No, I'm not," Blade said, disagreeing. "Oh, intellectually I might have seen the truth, but I never felt it in my heart. I would never admit there would always be violence. Always. Until all the power-mongers, the fanatics, and the psychopaths are eradicated from the *entire planet,* the Home will never be safe. The Family will face peril after peril."

"How does this relate to your decision?" Plato queried.

"Maybe it's time I took a look at the broader picture," Blade replied. "Maybe it's time I stopped being so selfish, thinking only of the Home. As Melnick mentioned, there are threats within the Federation we must deal with. And there are a lot of people in the Outlands and elsewhere who need our help. This Freedom Force Melnick has proposed could mean the difference between life and death for those unable to protect themselves."

"Does this mean what I think it means?" Plato asked.

Blade nodded. "I've decided to accept. Let Melnick and the others know. I will head the Freedom Force. I'll persuade Jenny to move to L.A. But I want one thing clearly understood."

"What?"

"I will run the Freedom Force my way," Blade stated. "I will select the ones under me. And I will have veto power over every mission. If Melnick and the rest can't accept my conditions, then they can forget it."

"They will accept," Plato said.

Blade glanced over Plato's shoulder and saw Hickok emerge from the hotel and walk toward them.

Plato turned. "Ahhh. Nathan is coming. I will convey your decision to the Federation leaders." He hurried off.

Blade saw Hickok and Plato exchange a few words, and then the gunman strolled over to him.

"Howdy, pard."

"Did you find any trace of him?" Blade questioned.

"Nary a whisker," Hickok answered. "Kraken has flown the coop. The Army is scourin' the amusement park, but they won't find him."

"We'll run into him again," Blade said. "I feel it in my bones."

"I reckon," Hickok remarked in a melancholy manner.

"What's wrong with you?" Blade asked.

Hickok looked into Blade's eyes. "Plato told me you've decided to take Melnick up on his offer."

Blade pursed his lips. "I've got to do it. You see that, don't you?"

"The Home won't be the same without you," Hickok commented.

"I'll only be gone for a year," Blade said.

"Yeah. Just a year," Hickok repeated, clearly depressed.

"I'll come to visit periodically," Blade stated. "It's not like I'm leaving forever."

Hickok averted his eyes and cleared his throat. "I hope Plato doesn't get all bent out of shape over your leavin'. You know how blamed wishy-washy he can be."

Blade grinned. "I know."

Hickok casually surveyed their immediate vicinity, insuring no one was watching.

Blade was about to head for the hotel when the gunman suddenly stepped forward and embraced him in a fleeting bear hug, then just as quickly stepped back, his thumbs hooked in his gunbelt.

"You ever tell anyone I did that," Hickok said gruffly, "and I'll shoot you in the foot."

"I won't tell. I promise."

"Good. Let's go grab a bite to eat," Hickok suggested.

Blade was experiencing an odd constriction in his throat. He coughed, relieving the tension. "I'm with you."

The two Warriors sauntered toward the glass doors.

"I've been thinkin'," Hickok said.

"About what?" Blade queried.

"The Family will need a new head Warrior," Hickok observed.

"That's right."

"I think I'll volunteer for the job," Hickok stated.

"You?"

Hickok glanced at Blade. "And why not, pard? They can't give the job to just anybody."

"No, they can't," Blade concurred.

"They need someone with a cool head on his

shoulders," Hickok stated. "Someone who's calm in any crisis."

"You?"

"Someone the rest of the Family respects," Hickok went on. "Someone who's a born leader."

"You?"

"Why do you keep sayin' that?" Hickok asked.

"No reason," Blade said, suppressing a grin.

"I sort of like the notion," Hickok declared.

Hickok as the head Warrior? Blade was boggled by the idea. "You think you could handle it, huh?"

Hickok chuckled. "Pard, it'd be a piece of cake!"

Blade will return to the series in ENDWORLD #14: SEATTLE RUN. Also look for Blade in a brand new series, BLADE #1: FIRST STRIKE, coming to bookstores in April, 1989.